Review

A journalist investigates a decades-old mystery.

"Great-aunt Milly shot a priest" is the family legend that propels this novel (after *Whidbey*, 2016) tale, and Maggie Callahan, who has heard this family remark all her life, is determined to see if there is any truth to it. Milly Miller was among many who were forced from their land and livelihood when the Grand Coulee Dam was built in the 1930s in Washington state. Off goes Maggie, a journalist, to search the parish records in Grand Coulee and then the diocesan records in Spokane. Bishop Davis starts stonewalling her, but she finds an ally in Father Matthew Brannigan, the young pastor of St. Francis parish in Grand Coulee. Father Matthew in turn has a friend in old Father Francesco in Spokane. They begin digging and start playing almost a cat-and-mouse game with Bishop Davis. Clearly the bishop is hiding something; then there is that secret archive storeroom—quite Gothic, really. In the midst of this, Maggie is called to report on a forest fire west of Grand Coulee. She does herself proud (she is search-and-rescue and EMT trained), saving a lost 6-year-old and a wayward horse. There is also much discussion with Father Matthew and Father Francesco about priestly celibacy (yes, readers can see where this is going). Finally she and Father Matthew track down an old, frail priest who was involved not with Milly but with her sister Evangeline, Maggie's grandmother. Brunjes spins her story effectively; the chapters are short and keep things moving. But the portrayal of Bishop Davis is a bit much. He never simply "says." Instead, he hisses, thunders, growls, sputters, and roars. He does have a lot to lose, so the near caricature is understandable. Nevertheless, the secret that drives the narrative is deftly handled. The author milks the reveal for all its worth, and this reader took breaks between later chapters to savor the suspense. Tales about the Roman Catholic Church—its traditions, its enigmas, its moral stances, and the lives of its clergy—have always fascinated readers, and Brunjes makes a lively contribution to this category.

Kirkus Reviews

A diverting and intriguing family mystery involving a priest.
Review by CatherineByCatherineon February 26, 2017

This was great! I've always been a little hesitant about reading books where religion is involved, but definitely don't let that stop you from reading this book.

The Last Confession begins with a story. Legend says that Maggie's great-aunt Milly shot a priest. But no one in Maggie's family explains why or how, and now Maggie is determined to figure out the truth. The journey to answers, though, is not that easy.

The plot for this was a wild ride; I loved how the story did not completely center around Maggie investigating the family legend. Along the way, we got to see glimpses of Maggie's job and family, and this allowed me to gain a very well-rounded perspective of her journey and everyday life. Maggie's path to the truth was extremely engaging. This was the type of mystery that I could completely immerse myself into, and I couldn't wait to get to the end.

I loved the characters - the protagonists were flawed but likeable, and the antagonists were very complex. It seemed as though every character had their own personalities and histories, and this really helped make the story seem realistic and seamless. Maggie, the main character, was someone who was headstrong and persistent, but not mindlessly so; she could hold her own in a debate, and she had her own opinions about gender issues and religious matters. I very much enjoyed reading the discussions she had with other characters about celibacy - there are endless clashes between tradition and modernity in the current political and social sphere, and I loved the glimpse of real world problems we got.

The writing style was very engaging, and I loved how the author set up the final reveal. The story was very well thought out, and the way the book was structured really made it a page-turner.

Overall, I would definitely recommend this for everyone who enjoys reading mystery. I promise you'll be hooked!

Maggie Callahan grew up knowing bits and pieces of her family history. Some true, and some questionable. One of those questionable pieces was that her great aunt had shot a priest. Not being to let go of this accusation, Maggie sets out to find the truth of it all. Her quest begins with the bishop of the Archdiocese of the town Spokane. Like most members of the Catholic Church, the bishop is willing to do anything to protect the church, including give Maggie a hard time. But, not all members were so tight lipped, and unwilling to help solve the mystery. Maggie finds a friend in Father Matthew and his willingness to help her. Will Father Matthew keeps true to his assignment of blockading Maggie with her search, or will he be the one to help solve her family's secret since around the 1930's?

"The Last Confession" by Author Pat Kelley Brunjes explores the Catholic concepts and law of Celibacy within Priesthood. The concept explores the long debated discussion of whether or not priest should remain taking a vowel of celibacy or come to terms with with the new age and way of such issues, and allow priest to marry and father children like many other religions, parishes, and even some Catholic Churches in other countries. Offering an intriguing, twisting plot of mystery and romance, and well developed characters, author Pat Kelley Brunjes, has given readers a true page turner.

To Judy
Hope you enjoy the read.
Love Pat

THE LAST CONFESSION

Pat Kelley Brunjes

C. 2017 by Pat Kelley Brunjes
Deer Lake Press, Puget Sound, WA
All rights reserved.

ISBN: 1539913023
ISBN 13: 9781539913023
Library of Congress Control Number: 2016918583
CreateSpace Independent Publishing Platform
North Charleston, South Carolina
Subjects: 1. Priests, fiction 2. Celibacy, fiction, 3. Confessions, fiction 4. Mystery, fiction 5. Romance, fiction
813.6
Printed in the United States of America
9 8 7 6 5 4 3 2 1
This is a work of fiction. Names, characters, places are either fictitious or used fictitiously as part of the story.

To Mike, Kathleen, Kate, Ian, Brendan, and Alexandra

CHAPTER ONE

"Great-aunt Milly shot a priest. Big freakin' deal, Maggie. It happened over seventy years ago, if it happened at all."

Maggie stood with hands on her hips, glaring at her younger brother, Lucas, who lounged in the recliner, long legs dangling over the footrest. He just didn't get it.

"You're some kind of obsessed," he added before she could get her breath to respond.

"Okay, so I'm obsessed," she sputtered, "but there's something I never told you, or anyone. Grandmother Callahan and Great-aunt Milly are always with me. They even come to me in my dreams and ask me to find the truth of what happened."

"You dream about our grandmother and great-aunt?" Lucas rolled his eyes. "That's bizarre."

"Bizarre or not, I'm haunted by the story that Milly shot a priest. And lately I'm starting to wonder if I'm being haunted by Grandmother. How many years have we been hearing about this? How many years has no one ever been interested enough to find out if it's even true?"

"I tune it all out. It's useless gossip. Why go on a useless mission?"

"I don't find it useless, Lucas. Besides, I need a vacation from work before I do bodily harm to Bruce." She wrinkled her nose at the mention of her despised coworker.

"It'd be cheaper to just hammer that jackass. I'd do it for nothing, but it's your dollar, Sis, not to mention your vacation time." Lucas kicked the footrest back and sat up straight in the chair. "What are you going to do?"

"I have an appointment with the bishop of the Spokane Diocese. He's agreed to meet me at the Church of St. Francis in Grand Coulee. I'll ask to look at church records."

"And you think a bishop is going to let you look at church files? You're kidding yourself."

"Perhaps, but I'm going to try," she said, brushing away some invisible lint on her sleeve.

"I'm just saying there are better ways to spend your vacation than running off to Grand Coulee to see if you can find out about a priest our great-aunt supposedly shot. You've spent a lifetime listening to a bunch of old dingbats in the family gossip chain without any facts to back up their theories. You're going to spend money on a wild goose chase and just be disappointed. Why don't you go bungee jumping in New Zealand or skydiving up in Snohomish? That would make way more sense than using your vacation time to traipse off across the mountains chasing ghosts."

Maggie stared into his dark brown eyes and grinned. She wasn't going to be talked out of her mission by a skeptical brother. "Why don't you come with me?"

"I don't have any desire to talk to stuffy old priests about history that has nothing to do with my life." He hesitated a beat before asking, "What do *you* think happened over there, anyway? Do you suppose the priest wouldn't let Milly use the church for a bake sale or a quilting bee? Or maybe something really wicked happened, like he came on to Milly. Or maybe he was doing the boys or maybe he was fooling around with little girls or maybe he made a pass at ol' Ben and she nailed him." Lucas smirked.

"Since all you want to do is ridicule me, I'm out of here," she snapped.

"Well, I'll grant that you are one determined lady. I hope you find what you're looking for." Lucas slammed his book closed and headed for the stairway. "Need a shower," he called over his shoulder as he took the stairs two at a time. "Got a date at Lake Sammamish."

Maggie watched him disappear. Her bratty little brother was in college now, pre-med, and thought he knew everything about the world. He was six years younger and when she was really irritated with him, she called him their parents' big mistake. But she knew if she ever needed help, he would be there. He was as lovable as he was annoying. She should have told him what their father had said in the hospital, following his heart attack.

"Come close, Maggie," Dad had whispered. "There is something I need to clear up about my Aunt Milly. She—" Before he could finish the sentence a massive stroke took him.

How she missed him, and she never stopped wondering what would have come after "she."

CHAPTER TWO

Mary Margaret Callahan sat in her car in front of the white frame church, her stomach churning. She gazed up at the steeple rising against a cloudless blue backdrop and thought about her love/hate relationship with the Catholic Church and how she arrived at such conflicted thinking. Intellectually, Maggie understood the conundrum. The pageantry, the ritual, and the history of the Mass captured her. It bothered her that her dislike of the church had been preprogrammed by family history. And why had she long felt suckered into believing a piece of family lore that might be false?

It boiled down to the fact that some family members truly believed her great-aunt, Milly, shot a priest. When she'd asked what happened, everyone talked around the question. She never got a straight answer, so she assumed they didn't know. Or they were hiding a secret.

Bringing her mind back to the moment, Maggie thought about what she wanted to learn. Was she on a fool's errand, as her brother suggested? She'd soon find out. She got out of the car and circled around the landscaped island in the parking lot with its signature statuary of St. Francis surrounded by woodland creatures. Bent at the waist, he held one arm out toward a charming plaster raccoon that was going to need its paint refreshed soon. Two squirrels were a bit oversized, but the doe and her fawn were perfect. St. Francis did have a settling effect on her uneasy nerves. She took a deep breath and walked across the driveway, through the carved white double doors into the church, searching for an office. When she found it, she knocked.

"Come in," called a strong baritone voice.

The room was huge, not the kind of office she expected to find in a small rural church. Bookcases lined the walls and the oversized mahogany desk did not seem to downsize it. Two tall, arched windows flanked a long wooden cross behind the desk which shone from years of polishing by the sleeves of priestly vestments. A carved wooden cigar box sat prominently on the left front of the imposing surface. Blue and scarlet oriental rugs added a luxurious note to the room. This was a room that spoke to Maggie of power and authority. She took an appraising look at the priest standing behind the desk. Who is this guy? she thought. He was much too young to be a bishop. And quite good-looking, she was embarrassed to note. Not stuffy at all, she would have to tell Lucas.

"My name is Maggie Callahan," she said in as confident a voice as she could muster. "I have an appointment with Bishop Davis."

The young man nodded and opened his mouth. Instead of giving him time to respond, she forged ahead, using her most professional demeanor. "I have family history connected to this church, Father, and I would like to have access to the church archives." There, it was out. Maybe too abruptly.

The priest's left eyebrow raised slightly, as if in response to the unusual request. As a young priest, new to the priesthood and his parish, he knew the records of the church were usually confidential.

"Could you be a little more specific about what you would like to know?" Before she could answer he added, "Incidentally, I'm Father Matthew Brannigan." He reached across the desk to shake Maggie's hand in greeting. His eyes twinkled in a warm smile.

Maggie shook his outstretched hand. Definitely not stuffy, she thought, but she wondered how much information to divulge to this obvious gatekeeper. Maybe she should insist upon taking her business directly to the bishop. Going straight to the top had always worked well for her. She squared her shoulders and said, "I'd really prefer to discuss this with the bishop, if you don't mind."

Father Brannigan's smile remained, but the eyebrow raised again, this time a little higher, signaling that he'd just met a rather haughty member of the Catholic flock. "By all means, Miss Callahan, I certainly don't mind, but the bishop had an emergency and was not able to drive over from Spokane to meet with you today. He asked me to offer his apologies and to deal with your concerns in his stead. This is my parish."

Maggie felt foolish. Her attempt to snub the young priest was enough to bring her nose out of the air. She relaxed her shoulders as she blurted out, "I believe my great-aunt, Mildred Miller, shot a priest here in the 1930s."

At this, Father Brannigan's smile turned into open-mouthed surprise. It was obvious that neither his new parish nor his new community had disclosed such a historic revelation to him. He restored his pastoral expression.

"And you believe the church has this in its records?" he asked.

"Yes. I mean I hope so. Priests don't get shot every day, you know."

Father Brannigan nodded his head in agreement, giving Maggie the encouragement she needed to spell out her mission and it began to spill out freely.

"I want to know what the priest did to get shot, and I want to know if my aunt did the shooting. I want to know what the church knows, and I believe it will be in the archives somewhere, I mean it just has to be. I've read all the Seattle newspapers for that time period. I figured if a priest was shot anywhere in the state, it would make a Seattle paper, don't you agree? But no—nothing. So if this really happened, and I believe it did, my only hope to get at the truth is to have access to the church records. I've been hearing about this all my life, and—"

"Whoa, Miss Callahan." Father Brannigan held both hands up to correct Maggie's breathless monologue. "This is a most unusual claim, the shooting of a priest. I'll have to run your request by the bishop before we go any further. And I must tell you, church records are generally not available to the public."

Maggie grimaced. "I was afraid I'd hear something like that. Surely you can make an exception." She clenched her teeth and scrutinized the young man across the desk from her.

"I'm really sorry, Miss Callahan." Father Brannigan's apology seemed genuine. "This is not like looking for a baptismal record or a marriage date." His tone bore witness to disappointment that he couldn't help this young woman who was so passionate about her mission.

"It's highly unlikely that Bishop Davis will allow a lay person to search through the records, but if you could give me more information about this alleged shooting, he might allow me to search on your behalf."

Father Brannigan gestured to the chair next to the desk. "Please, Miss Callahan, won't you have a seat and tell me more?"

Maggie inhaled a deep breath and sat down on the sturdy wooden chair as the priest sank into the plush chair behind the desk.

"All my life, whenever the family got together for any occasion, there was some allusion made about my father's aunt shooting a priest," she began. "They usually joked about it, but there was always an underlying sense that there was some truth to it.

It happened, I gathered, around the time when the government started building Grand Coulee Dam—between 1932 and 1935. For a long time I thought Milly might have done it because the priest sided with the government and tried to convince her to abandon her home to make way for the dam. They justified taking private property by calling it eminent domain." Maggie paused, her blazing eyes expressing the outrage Milly must have felt.

Father Brannigan looked across the desk at the indignant young woman and said, "I've been reading about the building of the dam. It's fascinating history, but I thought the federal government offered to buy the land from the people who lived near the river."

"That's true. They did pay the property owners," Maggie said. "But they weren't just taking her house—they were taking her livelihood. She fished for a living and she'd have to move off the river, and her a poor widow. But the point is, there was a priest connected to the stories I heard at the family dinner table every Thanksgiving and Christmas and he got shot. And the one thing the stories have in common is they all lived over here in this parish."

"I'm puzzled over why a priest would be shot for simply asking someone to move. It doesn't make a lot of sense."

"I agree," Maggie said. "That's why I'm determined to get to the truth. Through the years, I've heard the name 'Gregory,' but I've found no confirmation that any priest named Gregory was shot, let alone that Milly did it." She broke off to sneak a quick look at the priest across the desk from her, hoping she was convincing him to lobby the bishop on her behalf.

Father Brannigan shifted in the overstuffed desk chair and asked, "Does everyone in the family believe this story?"

Eagerly, Maggie went on. "My Grandmother Callahan always denied that Great-aunt Milly shot anyone, but then she always stuck up for her older sister, and Milly wasn't around to defend herself or to tell the real story. So whatever anyone said just seemed like gossip, but it drew me in like a magnet.

"After I combed the Seattle newspapers, I started to search the old newspapers in the Spokane Diocese. But all I got from it was a headache from reading microfiche in the bowels of the downtown Seattle library." Maggie grinned and was pleased to see the priest was smiling.

"So that's why I am asking for the church's assistance, Father Brannigan," she continued. "The time frame is short—only three or four years, so it shouldn't be too difficult." She hesitated for an uncomfortable moment and said, "Uh, please call me Maggie."

Father Matthew Brannigan looked as if he didn't know whether to be amused or unsettled by her forward suggestion. Amused won. "All right, Maggie," he laughed, "and you may call me Father Matthew, as do my parishioners." His expression turned serious. "Maggie, if Bishop Davis asks why you want to do this, what reason will you give?"

Maggie looked him straight in the eyes, calculating whether he would accept her truthful answer or whether she should try to couch it in her most diplomatic language. She decided on the safe answer. "Because Milly was a remarkable woman who deserves to be exonerated, once and for all."

She stopped and Father Matthew remained silent until Maggie felt uncomfortable. "Okay, I have to find out what happened."

Father Matthew leaned as far across the desk as he could toward Maggie, and his eyes held hers for a long moment. He watched Maggie brush stubborn auburn curls from her face in a nervous gesture.

"I sense there's more," he said.

"Yes," she admitted, drawing in her breath for a moment and holding it until she decided to share the rest of her reason. "But I'm not sure it would seem compelling to Bishop Davis."

"I am not Bishop Davis," he said. "Tell me." Maggie found herself telling him what she had not told anyone else, even her brother.

"On his death bed, my father tried to tell me something about his aunt, that would be Milly, but it was too late and he died. Shortly after that, she and my grandmother started coming to me in dreams to say I must get to the truth of this story. Grandmother says time is short."

Father Brannigan sat back in his chair and looked across the desk at the young woman who seemed sincere and quite sane.

"Really? You dream about them?"

"Yes I do, but mostly my grandmother. She walks toward me until her face is just inches away. She doesn't really say anything, but her eyes lock on mine and I try to back away, but I can't. And then, without words, she tells me not to give up because there's something I must do. I know it's Grandmother Callahan, but her eyes are young and it almost feels like I'm staring into my own eyes. In the past few weeks, her eyes tell me time is running out. That's why I'm here."

"And your great-aunt?" the priest asked,

"She is further away—in a field—waving me to come closer, and as I do, she turns and runs, as if she is leading me to something. I know if I follow I will find out what I need to know, but then she disappears and I'm left to find my way alone."

Father Matthew gave Maggie's stunning disclosure a few moments of respectful silence before he spoke.

"I've never been one to deny the power of dreams. After all, according to scripture many of the prophets received their revelations in dreams. But the bishop is the one who needs to be convinced, and I doubt that he will be impressed."

"He just has to approve a search. I can't imagine Great-aunt Milly shooting anyone, especially a priest. I think it just wasn't in her DNA to do such a thing. So someone should try and clear her name, and then we should try to find out what really happened." Maggie's voice carried the urgency and passion she felt.

Father Matthew settled a little deeper in the chair. His professors at the seminary hadn't talked about dealing with this kind of situation. "Why don't you tell me more about Great-aunt Milly?"

"She was a tough lady, but she loved her family, which was essentially her husband, Ben, who died when they were still quite young, and my Grandmother Callahan and her family. Milly never had children of her own. After she left Grand Coulee, she moved briefly to Spokane and then on to St. Maries, Idaho, and bought a small farm on the St. Joe River. I loved that place when I was a little girl. There were no roads into her house so she would row over in her boat and pick us up from the road. People did this for years. She was always known for helping her neighbors. Shooting someone just doesn't fit the picture I have of her." Maggie was on a high, buoyed by his interest.

"One of my favorite stories happened near the end of her life when she broke her leg coming back from the boat. She was in her eighties, living alone, milking the cow and caring for the horses. It was about three quarters of a mile from the house to the landing, across a huge field, up a hill to the railroad tracks, and then up another hill to the house. She pulled herself across the field, up to the railroad crossing, and set the red flag so the train would stop and find out what she needed—one of the conditions she had insisted on when the railroad wanted to cross her land. If it hadn't been for the railroad men, she probably would have died. No mobile phones in those days, you know."

"An impressive story, and an impressive lady," Father Matthew said. "But I'm still not sure we have enough for Bishop Davis to allow a search."

"I hope he will. Please, help me." Maggie folded her arms. "How long will it take before I get an answer? I only have a few days." Her tone was blunt.

"I should have an answer for you tomorrow. The bishop will be in town later today. If he allows it, I will do the search and then pass the information on to you. Is there a phone number where I can reach you?"

She dug in her purse and with a huge smile and a flourish, produced her business card. "I have a mobile phone because of the nature of my work," she said. "You can reach me any time." She could see her pride in the professional touch was not lost on Father Matthew. If she could have read his thoughts further, she'd have known he pondered on how he would handle such an odd request with his superior. He knew the bishop would not be happy and would think she was prying.

"I'll call you as soon as I have any information," he said. "Or better yet, come back tomorrow about two o'clock. I should know something by then."

Maggie gave him a small smile and offered her hand. "I'll be here. Thanks, Father." She turned and walked out the imposing door without looking back.

Father Matthew Brannigan watched her exit. Maggie Callahan was not a woman who would give up easily.

CHAPTER THREE

Bishop Davis arrived in early evening as the sun began to set, cloaking the dam in a warm glow. When Father Matthew arrived at the office, Bishop Davis was leaning back in his chair, sipping a scotch and water, his old Meerschaum pipe at the ready. "Excellency," Father Matthew greeted the bishop with a slight bow and then stood so rigid he looked to be standing at attention.

Bishop John Davis, in his black cassock, was an imposing man who had been a bishop for decades. He was known as a somber man, almost harsh as he went about his ecclesiastical duties. He demanded strict adherence to Church policy, including saying the Mass in Latin once a month. He also insisted that priests make every effort to work closely with their parishioners. But for all the show, he wasn't a nurturing soul. He ran the diocese like a military unit. In spite of a doctrine that demanded a public life of poverty, chastity, and obedience, he lived in a luxurious home in Spokane with a cook and housekeeper. He was known to offer the men of the parish an occasional cigar and sip of aged whiskey. When he travelled, he had apartments available to him on each parish campus. Expensive memorabilia he had picked up from his world travels decorated every apartment.

"I met with Miss Callahan as you asked, Excellency, and she wants to know if she can search through church files, or if we could look to find out if her great-aunt, Mildred Miller, shot a priest here at the time of the building of the dam, and, if so, who was the priest, and what were the circumstances?" Father Matthew stood straight-backed as he awaited an answer.

Bishop Davis lifted his considerable weight from the leather chair. His belly jutted forward, suggesting years of sitting behind a desk, no exercise, and too much fine cuisine and spirits. "Let me get this straight. She thinks her aunt shot a priest. Is that why she thinks she has a right to demand to search church files?" The tone of his voice boomed disapproval.

"Sir, she's asking, not demanding. She wants to know about family history. I told her that she, personally, probably would not be allowed access to the information, but that I would check with you." The bishop's belligerence made Father Matthew uneasy.

Bishop Davis scowled at his underling. "I will not allow this. Who does she think she is?" He towered over the desk. Father Matthew stepped back, but continued to meet his eye. "We do not allow lay people access to our files, Father Matthew. Period."

The younger priest looked intently at the bishop, as if debating how to deal with a tyrant. "I understand, Excellency. I have a suggestion, however, that would help her, but not allow her access. What if I searched the archives? If the incident is true, it had to have occurred in the mid-thirties. I would go through three or four years of church papers. There is good reason to believe there never was a priest shot at either Grand Coulee or Coulee Dam— uh, known as Mason City then, I believe."

"Uh huh," the bishop grunted in affirmation. Father Matthew continued laying out his case.

"Since nothing turned up when she searched old newspapers, I suspect nothing really exists. A shooting involving our diocese would have been carried in newspapers throughout the state. If I find something, I will report first to you before I tell her." He hoped this argument was convincing.

"Humph, that might be a way to put her off, but you won't find a thing." Bishop Davis walked around the desk and paced back and forth in front of the young priest. "No priest was ever shot here. I would have known. But if there is a shred of truth in the allegation, it could be explosive and hurt the Church. I cannot allow that. We must avoid scandal at all costs. I do not want outsiders poking into Church affairs. Do you understand me, Father Matthew?"

"Yes, Your Excellency."

"I am putting you in charge of Miss Callahan. You and you alone will go through the files. You are to be discreet. Is that understood? Heaven only knows what her real motives are." Bishop Davis reached into the pocket of his cassock and handed the young priest a cluster of keys, pointing out the one that opened the archives door. Then he returned to the leather chair and reached for his pipe and tobacco tin.

"Sir, I believe she just wants to know about family," Father Matthew mumbled, mostly to himself. Father Matthew wondered if the bishop really did know something but just didn't want to discuss it. He also wondered if the bishop carried all of the archive keys in the diocese and if all of the parish priests had to ask for them.

Father Matthew left the office briskly and went down the long hallway to a door that opened onto the side yard of the church. He approached the outside stairwell that led to the basement room where he would find the archives and then descended the narrow cement stairway. The key the bishop had shown him fit the heavy wooden door at the bottom of the stairs. He opened it and went inside the dark room. A light bulb hung from the ceiling, its chain almost out of Father Matthew's reach. In the room were stacks of boxes on shelves that lined the walls. He pulled all the boxes with date labels from 1933 to 1936. It took almost two hours to complete the search, checking every document for a clue. The bishop was right. There was nothing here. As he lifted the last box back into place, he noticed an iron door in the far back corner. He went over, tried the handle and found it wouldn't budge. He pulled the keys from his pocket and checked each one against the door. None worked. He searched the lintel for a key and then ran his hand over the wall searching for a nail. Finally he turned off the light and exited the room. The wooden door seemed heavier than before. He ascended the stairs and stepped into the early darkness of a Washington summer night. He knew Maggie would be disappointed.

CHAPTER FOUR

The afternoon had warmed up considerably. A slight breeze blew in from the coulee making the air feel like a body-sized hair dryer. Tiny dirt devils twirled about the dry terrain. Maggie arrived at the church promptly at two o'clock. She'd spent the day in a little makeshift museum–in-progress, looking at old documents and uncaptioned pictures of people who hadn't been identified yet. She'd found nothing to help her, not even people, as the museum was on the honor system with an unlocked door and a jar inviting visitors to put money in. She added five dollars and hid it among the few one-dollar bills that had probably been put in to seed the jar. No sense tempting the next visitor.

Father Matthew was waiting for her in the hall outside the office. Old pictures of saints hung on the beige walls. The saints seemed to be staring at them, watching their every move, asking questions. He motioned for her to sit in one of the brocaded antique chairs lining the hall. Their faintly musty smell reminded her of her grandmother's "company" room. She was pretty sure she knew why the two of them were sitting in the hall and who was sitting at the big desk behind the closed door. She flushed as a wave of resentment swept over her, along with embarrassment that she had shared the deeply personal fact of her dreams with a priest who was probably taking her for a ride. But she kept her composure.

They sat and Father Matthew said, "I'm sorry, Maggie, but as I expected, you cannot search the archives." His eyes seemed to express genuine regret. "I did get permission to search for you, but I'm sorry to tell you I found nothing that mentioned your great-aunt or a shooting that involved a priest. When I told Bishop Davis about the shooting, he insisted nothing like that ever happened here."

Maggie inhaled a deep breath and looked directly at Father Matthew, her eyes narrowed. "That's what I expected. The easy answer. Good for the Church, of course. We wouldn't want scandal. But it leaves me where the Church has always left me: on my own."

Father Matthew's eyes registered something more than regret. Shock, perhaps. Or empathy. It surprised her.

Maggie stood up. "Back to the microfiche, I guess. I don't know anyone who lives here, so there's no one I can approach who might have remembered my great-aunt."

Father Matthew responded with a new idea. "That may not be true. There is a gentleman in his nineties who comes to church every Sunday—Charlie Williams. He's in a wheelchair, but I would say his mind is still very much intact. If you like, I'll arrange for him to talk with you after Mass tomorrow. You'll be there?"

With that glimmer of hope Maggie brightened. "Yes, I'll be there. This is wonderful news. Thank you, Father. I appreciate the help more than you know." Energized, Maggie popped up from her chair, vigorously pumped Father Matthew's hand and headed for the door. This was maybe the most promising lead she'd had since she'd begun her quest. A real person who might have first-hand knowledge. She turned around halfway down the hall.

"Wow. Do you think we'll learn anything from this old gentleman? I hope so!" She swiveled back around and then turned again to wave goodbye on her way out the door. Father Matthew might easily have thought she seemed a bit like one of those whirling dirt devils of Eastern Washington on a summer day.

CHAPTER FIVE

Maggie woke early Sunday morning. She dressed and went downstairs to pick up her breakfast and greet her B and B hosts. Her room was tiny, but it looked down upon a beautiful garden with flowers ablaze. Maggie was amazed at how many small gardens dotted the town. I'll bet it wasn't that way before the dam came, she thought as she took her orange juice, muffin, and cup of coffee outside to sit on the wrought-iron bench. She may not have learned anything about Aunt Milly in her research, but she'd learned plenty about irrigation and the reclamation project. Not a dry subject, she quipped to herself.

The walk to the church was nearly a mile, most of it up steep hills. But she relished the time alone in the summer sun. She liked looking at the old buildings, wondering about their hidden stories, what skeletons they hid between their boards. And she looked forward to the panorama at the top of the hill—Banks Lake and its colorful canyon, the town climbing up the hillside in front of her, a little piece of Grand Coulee Lagoon glistening off to the right of the town, lovely even though she had learned at the museum it was actually a water treatment facility known among the locals as Poop Lagoon. The Church of St. Francis commanded an impressive view. She did not hurry.

For unexplained reasons, she was nervous about meeting Father Matthew. She had brushed her hair back and caught it with a clip, using a little more care than usual.

The Mass inspired her. The bishop had acted as the assistant, leaving the saying of the Mass to Father Matthew. The atmosphere felt very different from when she drove up to the church two days ago. It was warm and inviting. She credited Father Matthew for that and wondered if more people were now attending Mass as compared with the priest who had served before him.

After Mass, Father Matthew removed his vestments, and went out to mingle with the congregation in his priestly black shirt, black slacks and crisp white collar. He waved at Maggie when he saw her waiting and said, "I'm sorry that Bishop Davis was so adamant about releasing documents to you, Maggie. Not that I found any documents to release," he added.

"Hopefully, I'll learn more from Mr. Williams than I did from the newspapers, which have been a giant bust so far. I spent a fruitless afternoon on a microfiche machine at the library after I left you yesterday. I read about plenty of fighting and even some killings. Interesting enough, but nothing to help my search. The only priest I ran into was Father Gregory McCloud who seemed to be a pretty good guy—old, but alive and well in Corpus Christie, Texas and definitely not gunned down. The only thing relevant to my aunt was how she helped build the Indian school. Apparently she did a lot of good for this community. Oh, I do hope Mr. Williams remembers her."

Charlie Williams didn't look to be in his nineties except that he was frail and in a wheelchair. His gray hair, what little remained, was neatly trimmed. He carried a cane which suggested he could walk, but he apparently chose to be pushed on Sunday mornings.

He sported a beard which, according to Father Matthew, he had reportedly kept neatly trimmed for fifty years.

The parish hall at St. Francis had tables to seat a hundred people. Father Matthew wheeled the old man up to a table. Maggie smiled and offered Charlie her hand. "Hi. I'm Maggie Callahan and I'm so happy to meet you." A very strong handshake for someone so frail, she thought.

Charlie Williams looked up at the young woman and smiled appreciatively at the chance to meet someone under the age of 70 who wanted to talk to him about when he was young. That was a novel event in his life. "The pleasure is all mine, young lady." He looked as if he truly meant it.

"May I get you a cup of coffee and a cookie? Father, may I get you a cup, too?" Without waiting for an answer, Maggie turned toward the refreshment table.

"You may, but that's really my job," Father Matthew said.

"I'll get it this time," she called back over her shoulder as she headed for the big coffee urn and the people lined up in front of it. Maggie smiled. It pleased her to do this for Father Matthew.

Charlie Williams shouted, "Young lady you can get me two cookies. Any type as long as it's chocolate." He turned to Father Matthew and explained, for probably the hundredth time, "My wife, Bertha, used to make at least two types of chocolate cookies every Saturday. I've never given up my hankerin' for chocolate."

"How about cream and sugar for the two of you?" Maggie asked as she delivered the cookies and prepared to go back to pick up the coffee she'd poured. The priest shook his head.

"I like mine black," Charlie said. "Doesn't keep me awake at night. I can sleep through anything. Bertha used to tell me a burglar could come in the house and I'd sleep through it. I like my coffee black and my whiskey straight. My Bertha, God rest her soul, could take a sip of black coffee at noon and be walkin' up the walls all night." They all laughed.

"Be right back with three black coffees," Maggie promised.

Shifting his focus to Father Matthew, Charlie said, "So she wants to know what I remember about ol' Milly?"

"Yes, she wants to know about her family history and what it was like when they were building the dam."

Maggie returned with a tray of coffee to which she'd added chocolate cupcakes, much to Charlie Williams' delight. He grabbed one of them and set it aside.

"All right little lady. Father Matthew says you want to know about your aunty and the dam and what happened back then." He snagged three cookies in a single pass. "I remember your aunty and uncle like my own parents. Wonderful people. They sometimes took care of me and my sister when we were younger and our folks were away. In fact, I was named after your uncle Ben—Charles Benjamin Williams, that's me. I learned how to fish from Milly. I couldn't net like her and the Indians because until I was about fifteen, I couldn't hold the net. If I'd caught a fish, me and the net would've been in the river. I used a pole, though, and caught my share of fish," he assured them.

"Sounds like a good childhood to me," Father Matthew observed, reaching for a cupcake.

"Good Catholic woman, too, your great-aunty—she helped out ol' Father Gregory all the time. She was known for raising money to build the school on the reservation. She'd tell people in church they had to tithe twice, once for the church and once for the school. They got it built in about four years. Paid for it as they went along, thanks to your aunty. She thought those Indian kids should go to school close to home, but that's a whole 'nother piece o' history." Maggie knew he was referring to the boarding schools Indian children were forced to attend. She was happy to hear Milly opposed it—another example of her good heart.

Charlie went on. "What Milly was really known for was her work when the dam was being built. Here was a lone woman who provided most of the fish for the town. 'The B Street Provider' they called 'er. Ben was gone by then." Charlie paused long enough to dunk a cookie in his coffee.

"What was B Street?" Maggie had read of this street in her research, but it hadn't come up in the family stories. She wanted to know more.

"It's a street here in Grand Coulee where the men hung out when they weren't workin'. There were restaurants and bars, and a couple dance halls. But the main attraction was all the women living on B Street—they'd migrated to the dam, and I guess you know why." Charlie flashed a knowing look at the priest and the young woman. "They waited for the men to get off work and then showed 'em a good time. They'd meet 'em at the dance halls and then take 'em back to their rooms. What the men didn't spend on whiskey, they spent on women. Makes you wonder how much money actually got back to their families."

"Maybe most of the men didn't have families," Father Matthew suggested.

Charlie looked at Father Matthew with an expression that clearly questioned the priest's level of worldly understanding. "Maybe. There were a few homes built for the workers' families, but not many. Over the years I learned that some family women worked the streets in order to have money to feed their kids."

Father Matthew spoke up again. "I can't imagine women with children actually working the streets."

The old man looked sharply at the priest in a way that said maybe this man didn't understand being poor.

Maggie wondered silently, Is this priest naïve, or does he just prefer to put the best face on human behavior? She decided on the latter.

Charlie picked up the story line. "A lot of the Indians who worked on the dam lived on B Street, too. They were accepted there, but not in the towns. Some who weren't hired on at the dam worked in restaurants and helped the local farmers during the summers.

"Milly delivered fish a couple o' times a week to restaurants and individual families. Sometimes I helped 'er. It was tough for her to carry the fish by 'erself even though she had a small cart and an old horse. A couple of Indians used to help her carry fish up from the river. I think she had a pretty good business."

"What years were those?" Father Matthew asked as he ate a second cupcake.

"Had to 've been between 1930 and 1935 or '36. Actually, she fished during the early years they worked on the dam and it was well underway by '35. Finished about 1939, but she was gone by then."

Maggie looked at Father Matthew and saw intensely blue eyes that were puzzled. "That doesn't make sense," he said. "By 1935, if the dam was well under construction, she would have been off her property and yet you say she maintained a fishing business through those years. She must have been living somewhere else."

"Bingo!" Charlie said. "Sharp thinkin', Father Matt. She went upstream with the Indians when her house went under, and then she moved to town and lived in a tiny white house with a white picket fence out front, one of those houses she said she'd never own. One year I whitewashed it for her, the fence that is. She still fished upstream, though. How about another cup o' coffee?"

Maggie stood to get more coffee, glad that the young priest put up no objection this time. As she turned toward the back of the room, she saw Bishop Davis, still in his white chasuble and black chimera, watching her. She wondered how long he had been standing there and why he didn't come into the hall.

When she returned, Charlie said, "You know, when you were talkin' about a shooting taking place here, I'm not sure one ever happened, at least her doin' it. Oh, I'm not sayin' it wasn't a rough time. Lots o' violence, but most of it was men drinkin' to let off steam over women and bad poker games. Y' know, their day jobs were things like haulin' buckets of cement on their backs up a cement mountain. Don't think I could've ever hung by pulleys and ropes down the side of a five hundred foot cement slab."

"Me either," said Father Matthew. "It would take some guts to do that, and to dig into rock and plant dynamite."

Maggie looked out the window and changed the subject. "Where did the dam administrators live?"

"Good question." Charlie leaned forward and picked up a fourth cookie. "They lived apart from the laborers. Mostly in Mason City—you call that Coulee Dam now—over with the engineers. They had bungalows and kept to themselves. Their kids were isolated from the workers' families, except in school. That's where we all pretty much learned to get along with each other. But up on B Street, that was somethin' else."

"True," Maggie agreed. "So you don't think my great-aunt was involved in a shooting."

"Especially if she'd shot Father Gregory," Charlie conceded. "I was just a kid, but I'm sure I would have remembered that 'cause Milly was a friend. What I remember is Milly doin' things for the community. Even if she resented, maybe even hated the dam, she was always a good soul."

"So maybe she didn't shoot a priest. Maybe it's all family gossip, after all. I'm glad to know she was kind to everyone, especially the Indians." Maggie looked at Charlie and marveled at the old man's memory.

"Yep, they loved her. I remember when the Indians had to leave Kettle Falls. They had a big shindig to say g'bye to their stompin' grounds. They'd dug up their ancestors' bones and moved 'em over to the Colville Reservation, and then when the water got to their doorsteps, they moved, too. The reason I mention it is because it would've been a real honor to be invited to that shindig, and Milly was there—the only white woman. I saw a picture of it, and there she was. Maybe you can find that picture at the museum. 'The Ceremony of Tears' they called it. I remember it 'cause it seemed pretty sad, even to a snot-nosed kid."

Maggie nodded her head and remembered seeing a picture at the museum labeled "Ceremony of Tears." She would have to go back to look for Milly's white face among the sea of handsome bronzed faces. She lifted her eyes to the ceiling, pondering the many sacrifices that went into the building of Grand Coulee Dam.

Charlie finished his coffee and put the empty cup on the table. "I gotta go, my legs are hurtin' and my ride is waitin'. Could you wheel me out, Father? I don't suppose I helped you much, Maggie, but I enjoyed talkin' about the dam. If I think o' something else, I'll call Father." He stopped and contemplated for a moment. "Oh, wait. There is one more thing. Don't know if it'll help, but Milly finally moved to Spokane. Her sister, Evangeline, went there to find a job. Can't remember exactly when Milly moved, but I remember she sold everything she had, including the old horse. She took the old McClellan saddle with her, though. It was Ben's army saddle. I really wanted that saddle," he sighed. "Later, she moved up the St. Joe River in Idaho."

"Thanks, Charlie. I know about her place on the St. Joe River, but I don't know much about her time in Spokane. I remember the saddle. I wanted it too, but forgot to ask for it. Looks like we both lost on that one. I hope we'll get to talk again." Maggie reached over to hug Charlie and kiss his weathered cheek, thinking she might want to extend her holiday. "Perhaps next Sunday."

After he had taken Charlie out to the parking lot where a parishioner waited, Maggie watched Father Matthew join the bishop and walk out the back door toward the rectory. She couldn't help being irritated by this game they played. The bishop and Father Matthew had discussed the details of her quest privately. She was odd person out. Information that came from Father Matthew had to be filtered and maybe edited by the good bishop. I wonder what they are talking about right now, she thought as she turned to leave by the front door.

CHAPTER SIX

The two priests walked in heavy silence until the bishop spoke. "I don't suppose she learned anything from the old man." Bishop Davis said it as if he already knew the answer.

"No, she didn't or at least nothing that she didn't already know. I'm sure she's frustrated because nothing she heard growing up seems to be true. I'm not sure what she will do now." Father Matthew set his jaw and followed the bishop with little enthusiasm until they reached the aggregate walk leading to the front porch of the modest frame house. Nothing on the outside divulged the luxurious suite inside which had been added on to accommodate the bishop's visits to the parish.

Bishop Davis turned to face the young priest. "I want to put an end to this, but I know that eventually she is going to want to go to Spokane to look into the files there, so I suggest you tell her to go ahead. I don't want her reporting that she was stonewalled by the Church."

Father Matthew showed surprise. "Her question will be, 'Will the old files in Spokane be any different from the old files in Grand

Coulee?'" It was Father Matthew's question also. "What shall I tell her?"

The bishop scowled. "Tell her whatever you want!" he snapped. "You can look through the files for her like you did here in Grand Coulee. You are to be her liaison. Like I said before, I want you with her. I don't want her collecting information without your knowledge. In Spokane she will learn that nothing questionable exists, and then she'll stop her snooping."

Bishop Davis paused, and folded his arms over his chasuble in a thoughtful pose before he went on. "I want you to question her about what she may already know. Ask her what the family talked about. Find out what she thinks may have happened. Again, I want to know everything, not only from our files, but also what she finds out from the newspapers and any other source she might dredge up." Bishop Davis climbed the steps and entered the house, leaving Father Matthew staring at his retreating figure.

Father Matthew half bowed and hurried back to his office in the church. He dialed Maggie's mobile. She answered and said she was in the church side yard near a charming replica of Dolfi's "The Risen Christ."

"The sweet smell of honeysuckle permeates the air. I'm going to sit here awhile to read and breathe pure fragrance."

"I'll be there in a few minutes. Please don't leave." Father Matthew scribbled a note on a piece of paper, folded it, and put it in his pocket, then hurried toward the door that led to the garden.

He arrived and sat next to Maggie. "You're right about the honeysuckle. It takes my breath away. I don't spend as much time paying attention to nature as I would like." He looked at the book lying open on her lap. "What are you reading?"

"*Fear of Flying.*"

"Isn't that a racy book?"

"Oh, I suppose. I decided to read it because a friend who teaches a class called 'Introduction to Flying' told me the high school librarian bought thirty copies for him to use. He almost fell off his chair telling me. I had to read it to find out what the hullaballoo was about."

"Sounds like the librarian doesn't read books or reviews." Turning to look at the young woman sitting next to him, he said, "I have good news. The bishop has opened up a new venue to the hunt. Can you drive to the diocese headquarters in Spokane? It's about ninety miles. The bishop will allow me to search the archives there, but you'll have to make a formal request like you did in Grand Coulee. I told the bishop I was sure you would. Can you get there tomorrow morning?"

Maggie's mouth opened wide in surprise and she clapped her hands together in celebration. "That's wonderful!" Her face, shining with hope, turned wary. "But why would we find anything there that we didn't find here? What about the bishop? What's his agenda? I have to admit he scares me a little. It feels like he's the chess master and I'm a pawn. What if you do find something? Will he allow you to tell me?" Distrust was creeping into her anticipation, but this was still a breakthrough and she smiled grudgingly.

"I think he'll let me tell you about whatever I find, but I must tell him first." With that, Father Matthew handed Maggie the scribbled note and said, "Here are the directions to Holy Names Cathedral where the diocese offices and archives are located. As soon as you get there, go to the diocese office and request permission to access the files. You will be told again that you can't have access, but that I have been named to do it for you. Then find something to do for a few hours. Maybe more microfiche?" He chuckled.

Maggie sighed. "You know, I came to the church looking for assistance, but it doesn't feel like I'm getting any help except from you. Cynic that I am, I don't see the bishop willingly giving up any information. Sorry, Father, it's just that I'm not convinced the man really wants to help me."

Father Matthew laughed and said, "You're not a cynic. If you haven't read Dante's *Inferno*, I suggest you read it to get an idea where these attitudes come from."

Maggie leaned toward him and whispered, "I've read it. It beats *Fear of Flying*." Then she sat up straight. "Furthermore, I understand the nine circles of Hell that are supposed to lead us to God. I love the story, but it's an allegory, and I don't believe in the point Dante was trying to make. And I don't believe Bishop Davis has ultimate control over whether I get to heaven. He can, however, make my immediate life pretty frustrating. He acts as if there is a deep, dark secret that he doesn't want me to find."

"Keep the faith, Maggie. It was his idea that you should know what's in the diocese archives so maybe he's not all bad, and I'm here to help you find out what the Church knows. I'll call you on your mobile phone when I have something to report—probably late afternoon. Travel safely." With that, Father Matthew stood, smiled at Maggie and returned up the path toward the church. Maggie folded her arms and watched him disappear around the corner, hoping he would turn and offer a parting wave. He didn't. She stashed *Fear of Flying* in her voluminous carryall and left.

CHAPTER SEVEN

The next morning the sun edged through the narrow church windows, creating a saintly glow for early prayers. Father Matthew assisted Bishop Davis at the seven o'clock Mass, distracted by thinking about his conversation with Maggie. In spite of what he'd told her, he suspected she would get the same negative response in Spokane that she'd gotten here. Bishop Davis headed the diocese and Father Matthew was obligated to do as he was told.

Father Matthew saw Bishop Davis as a dichotomy. He constantly told his priests they must strive for self-improvement, pray, and teach that a relationship with God must be internalized, that all people must work to understand the meaning of God, humble themselves and help others.

But Father Matthew had seen Bishop Davis in his dark moments, when he viewed anyone who questioned the church or his authority as evil or unworthy. He was a disciplinarian right out of a Dickens novel. It was his Achilles heel, in the young priest's opinion. And the bishop certainly viewed Maggie as out of order for asking questions.

Father Matthew studied the stained glass windows, tried to read the Biblical stories and faces of the saints for some direction. He prayed for patience and inspiration.

Mass over, Bishop Davis returned to the rectory and prepared for his return to Spokane. "My boy," he called to Father Matthew, "my bag is ready."

The young priest dutifully entered the guest suite to fetch the suitcase and the clothing bag that held the bishop's vestments. The bishop was never willing to give up those princely garments for the more ordinary robes available at the parish churches.

"Why don't we ride together on this beautiful morning?" Bishop Davis was giving an order, not asking a question. "I would like to sit back and take in the scenery. You will drive the Town and Country."

"Of course, Your Eminence," Father Matthew agreed, even though it meant he would not have a car in Spokane and would have to find a ride back to Grand Coulee. He thought of Maggie's words. He, too, often felt like a pawn.

The drive to Spokane took two hours. Father Matthew drove while the bishop stared out the window. Conversation was limited to a discussion of the heat, notwithstanding the air conditioner kept the car at a cool seventy-two degrees, and what Father Matthew was to do when he looked in the Spokane archives on behalf of Maggie Callahan. Over and over the bishop told him he could look only in files from 1933 to 1936.

"Yes, Eminence," said Father Matthew, knowing he would extend his search in spite of the bishop's orders. Again, he wondered what damaging evidence the bishop thought he would find. Why limit the search to those three years?

When they arrived at the cathedral, Father Matthew parked the Town and Country in the covered garage beside the east tower where the bishop's office was housed. "I'll take your bags to the residence," he said after he walked the bishop to the massive wooden door and opened it for him. The bishop nodded his assent.

As he usually did, Father Matthew stopped to take in the majesty of Holy Names Cathedral, built of granite, its towers and spires rising gloriously from the center of the city's industrial park. A contrast in architecture and purpose, but strangely harmonious in spirit, the cathedral reaching out with beauty and inspiration to the smokestacks and the machines and the many souls who worked them.

Even more glorious, in the young priest's opinion, were the grounds—a fourteen-acre campus of lawns and gardens woven around the cathedral and its auxiliary buildings, with walking paths and secluded wooded niches for prayer and meditation. He pulled the bags, including his own, from the car, locked it, and headed down one of the paths to the residence, an imposing structure with a stone façade and wrap-around stone porch. Bishop Davis had remodeled the old house and added the façade to match the tone of the cathedral, while the interior was a study in modern convenience and decor. The housekeeper answered the bell and took Father Davis's luggage inside.

Visiting priests were housed in a building behind the Holy Names School, and Father Matthew took the roundabout path there, stopping at one of his favorite spots—a shaded bench beside the duck pond which accommodated a swan family as well. Two cygnets swam with their mother, the pen. Dad was nowhere in sight. Just as well, as Father Matthew once had words with the cob who took offense and the priest ended up jumping a hedge to avoid being nipped by a swan.

No time to visit with the wildlife today. Father Matthew dropped his overnighter inside the dormitory door and took the most direct path back to the church. When he arrived, he learned Maggie had already been there to ask for permission to search the diocese archives. Bishop Davis grudgingly stretched out his hand with the keys. "You will find the files in the chancery basement," he said. Father Matthew took the keys, acknowledged he would return them to the bishop's hand immediately following his search, and left the offices. The chancery was connected to the cathedral by a covered walkway affectionately dubbed The Cloister, lined on both sides with bright impatiens and geraniums. Father Matthew swept down The Cloister and unlocked the chancery's French doors.

The main hall of the chancery was a pleasant room that showcased an array of church artifacts and documents that dated back to the earliest missionaries. The archivist had a talent for design and display worthy of a museum curator. Too bad, Matthew thought, that the chancery was off limits to the public and only members of the clergy, nuns, and laypersons with special permission were allowed to view the exhibits. In the interest of time, he resisted the temptation to look over the collection. He knew it contained nothing that would help Maggie Callahan. Instead, he walked through the arch at the back of the room to an alcove where he found two doors. This was uncharted territory. He opened one and found a gleaming, well-lighted restroom. Behind the other door he found a very dark stairway, not at all inviting. When he flipped the light switch he could see an equally uninviting massive wooden door at the bottom of the stairs. Reminded of the basement in his own church, he descended and put the key into the iron lock. He turned it, listening for the clicks that indicated the tumblers had fallen into place. It took all of his strength to pull open the door. Nobody has to worry about stolen documents, he mused. A thief couldn't open the door without assistance. The musty odor of inattention greeted him. Apparently the archivist doesn't get down here much, he observed.

The room filled the full footprint of the chancery, large and lined on all four walls with shelves. Additional islands of shelving nearly filled the center space. On the shelves were dated boxes.

Lots of records, Father Matthew thought, and he made a mental note to learn more about the history of the Spokane Diocese.

Ignoring the bishop's instructions, he pulled fifteen boxes from the shelves, starting with January, 1930 and ending with December, 1939. He brushed away years of dusty neglect and sat down to confront his mission of discovery. It felt like a television drama.

The hours ticked by and occasionally he felt the need to stand and stretch his back. One by one he perused the contents of each box, then one by one he returned the fifteen boxes to their place of rest wondering about the last time they had been pulled from their shelves. He had found nothing that would interest Maggie Callahan.

As he walked toward the door, he noticed an iron door along the back wall, opposite the stairway. Flanked closely by shelves with more recently dated boxes, it had almost escaped his notice. It was similar to the one in Grand Coulee. He walked over and pulled the handle. It didn't budge. He put the key in the lock; it didn't turn. He looked around to see if another key hung nearby. Nothing. His sleuthing had been remarkably unproductive. So much for a cold case investigation.

Deep in thought, Father Matthew pulled the wooden door closed, locked it, climbed the stairway, and emerged into the late afternoon light of August shining through the chancery windows. He blinked several times and left the building to return to Bishop Davis's office.

"Eminence, I found nothing in the boxes from 1933 to 1936, but I do have a question. There is a small iron door on the back wall. It's similar to the door I saw in Grand Coulee. Could there be other files in that room?"

Bishop Davis swung around and gave Father Matthew a cold stare that told him he was overstepping his bounds. "Those rooms are private. They don't hold anything of importance or significance to your search."

Like an epiphany, Father Matthew knew exactly what they held. They held information about priests. In all his searching that afternoon or before, in his own church, he had never once come across any documents related to priests. There were no resumes, no priests' evaluations, nothing that would shed light on the business of being a priest in the Spokane Diocese. This was puzzling.

After giving up the keys and being summarily dismissed, Father Matthew walked back to the duck pond to sort out his dilemma. He was sure the bishop had the key to that iron door—and the iron door in the basement of St. Francis, as well. Short of burglarizing His Eminence's office and the residence, how could he get beyond those doors? He was reviewing how to handle dynamite when an idea struck him. His old friend, Father Francesco, had been assigned to this church for decades. Maybe he had a key. Or did he, too, have to ask the bishop for permission to enter the archives? Father Matthew left the pond and headed for Father Francesco's cottage.

One piece of Holy Names' history Father Matthew knew about was the humble beginnings of his friend's house—a tiny, hobbit-like brick dwelling tucked into a far corner of the campus, with an unruly spread of herbs and wild flowers for a front yard and a three-foot strip of gravel for a back yard, butted up against a chain link fence. It had been the first rectory, now the home of the semi-retired priest who currently served the Vatican as a writer of policy papers. The young priest loved Father Francesco as much as he loved his own father, and the old priest thought of Father Matthew as he would the son his profession denied him.

Father Francesco was in the garden trying to extract a few sprigs of rosemary from a tangle of vetch that had overrun the herb. He spied his young friend from a distance and hobbled down the gravel path to greet him. They hugged each other heartily.

"Matthew, I did not know you were in town! I am harvesting some herbs for pasta sauce. How about sharing my humble meal with me?"

"Not today, Father. I'll be meeting with a parishioner. Well, not really a parishioner—a young woman who—well, let's go inside and I'll explain."

Once inside the cottage, Father Matthew explained about Maggie Callahan and the dilemma of the iron door. The old priest sat quietly, his head bowed. Finally he looked up and said, "I do not have a set of keys, I'm sorry to say, but have patience, my young friend. I will help you find a way." There was something in Father Francesco's face that spoke of his knowledge of Maggie's quest that went beyond Matthew's level of understanding. Or his explanation.

CHAPTER EIGHT

Maggie was disappointed when Father Matthew told her he'd found nothing in the archives that mentioned anyone in her family or a shooting involving a priest. Her frustration level was rising by the minute and was beginning to show. She seemed to be wasting time and money chasing after something that apparently did not exist, but she wasn't ready to admit her brother might be right. Besides, Grandmother Callahan had appeared last night, just in time to boost Maggie's resolve. But she chose not to mention it to Father Matthew.

"I haven't eaten all day. Let's get a sandwich and walk down by the river," Father Matthew suggested, suggesting sympathy for this determined young woman who so doggedly searched out the truth of her family stories. "Maybe we can think of another approach."

"Do you have time? Don't you have churchly responsibilities? I shouldn't take more of your time," Maggie wearily protested.

"Nothing pressing until vespers. After all, the bishop instructed me to assist a parishioner, which is what I'm doing. I am getting concerned, however, about being away from my parish and will have to talk to the bishop about how long I am expected to assist you."

At that Maggie smiled and agreed. "I don't want to keep you from your duties. But, I am hungry."

"There's a deli about a half mile down, just after we get on the river path." Father Matthew's smile hinted at how pleasant it would be to have an early dinner with a bright young woman.

As they walked toward the river her mind raced from thought to unrelated thought. Maggie debated about what she wanted to ask the priest. She had spent the day making inroads through the *Spokesman-Review* archives, looking up both her great-aunt and her grandmother. Of course nothing had shown up. But she was curious about more than just her family. She wanted to ask him questions about Church policy and faith, but probably wouldn't because she did not want him to ask her questions about her own faith. And so her mind sprinted from one idea to another.

They found the deli and ordered generous sandwiches that would serve as dinner for both of them. Then they walked along the path until they found a bench overlooking the river. The Spokane River was placid until it dropped into Spokane Falls and then it became turbulent. In the distance a clock tower was visible so people always knew the time. Wild flowers sprang up everywhere.

"Do kayakers ever run the falls?" Maggie eventually asked, making a stab at small talk.

"They do. I've always wanted to do that, myself. Maybe someday." Switching gears, Father Matthew asked, "Maggie, what do you think happened regarding your great-aunt? What do you believe was never said at the dinner table?"

"I've thought a lot about that. My first thought is pedophilia. It seems the most likely reason someone would resort to shooting another person when the church is involved, but it's a subject that's never addressed in polite company, especially within the church. And truthfully, no one in the family ever suggested it. Milly never had any children but she would be the first one to defend someone else's child, if need be."

Father Matthew turned toward Maggie. "Remember what old Charlie said about Father Gregory trying to talk to Great-aunt Milly about selling out? He said she finally moved from Grand Coulee, so what about another priest?"

"What do you mean?" Maggie brushed her hair back with one hand and looked at Father Matthew.

"What do we really know about Father Gregory? He doesn't seem the sort to get himself shot. I'm saying you traced him from Grand Coulee all the way to Corpus Christie and you couldn't find anything. Nothing in the newspapers, nothing from the sheriff's office, and nothing from the one person still alive that knew him. I found nothing in my church records that implicated either Mildred Miller or Father Gregory in wrongdoing. The same was true here in Spokane. So my question is: What about another priest, perhaps a priest in another town? Maybe we are missing something. What about a priest at the church your grandmother went to?"

Maggie furrowed her brow at this new idea.

"Think about it, Maggie. Charlie said he did not believe your great-aunt would shoot a priest. What he did say, however, was that Milly used to go to Spokane as often as she could, to stay with her sister, your grandmother. But what if there was another reason Milly went to Spokane? And didn't Charlie say she finally moved over to Spokane and then at some point moved on to St. Maries, Idaho?"

"I never thought it might have happened somewhere else. The family talk always centered on the dam." Maggie began to trace the sequence of events in her aunt's life, trying to see how this new notion might fit the overall picture. "Let's see. Milly was widowed in 1930 at about age twenty-five when Uncle Ben slipped off the rocks and fell into the Columbia rapids. His body was recovered three days later, two miles down-stream. The Indians who were with him hunted for hours, hoping to find him before he died from exposure in the frigid waters, but obviously they failed.

"Milly buried him in the Catholic cemetery in Grand Coulee. Then she went home and struggled to survive. For a couple of years she lived in the home that she and Uncle Ben had built with their own hands. It sat at the river's edge on a forty-acre plot of rocky ground that was good for fishing but not much else. They cleared enough rocks so they could grow root crops and other vegetables. She canned the produce and salted or dried the fish to carry her through the cold winter months. In a good season she sold her extra vegetables, along with the fish, to the local restaurants. Dad said she had a tiny nest egg that she guarded with her life."

"She was a resourceful woman," Father Matthew murmured.

"What Milly knew most about was how to fish. The Indians continued to help her, making sure she had enough to survive the harsh winter months. Her neighbor, Tom, walked over every other day or sent his boys to make sure she was all right. Old Charlie must be one of those boys. It was a hardscrabble life, but she clung to that plot of land next to the Columbia River. Mildred Miller wouldn't have had it any other way."

"I get this part of the story," Father Matthew said. "But I still think we're missing something. What happened when the government got serious about building a dam? Did anyone threaten her?" He continued to search for paths not yet explored.

"Not that I know of. I never heard anything like that. Of course there was a lot of talk about the dam—you know not everybody was in favor of it, according to Dad. He wasn't even born when they built the dam, but his own father had worked on it in the early days, before he married Grandmother Callahan. When his father died of meningitis, Dad was about fifteen, so he went out looking for work. He and Grandmother Callahan lived in Spokane, but he tried to get a job at the dam. He was too young, though, and they wouldn't hire him. Sorry, I'm getting sidetracked."

"So you don't know if anyone ever threatened Milly?" he asked, steering her back to the current speculation.

"I'm not sure. I know she talked a lot against the dam."

"So it was more than Milly not wanting to surrender her land. She was opposed to the dam?"

"Definitely. It would destroy fishing and fishing was the livelihood for her and the Indians."

Father Matthew reflected. "I can understand why people took the cash and moved off their land. It gave them security, something many of them had never known, according to the story you tell." Maggie looked at him sharply. Was he taking the side of the Feds?

He went on. "She must have been one very tough lady to stand up to the federal government for as long as she did."

That eased Maggie's suspicions. She kicked off her shoes and flexed her toes. "About three thousand people were uprooted, you know. The Indians had to move again, this time to the Colville Reservation. Milly's friends encouraged her to move into Grand Coulee or Mason City, but she was not much for town living with lots of people, stores, animals, kids and whirling dust blowing through her house and up her nose. Besides, there were no houses available. People looking for work took homes and rooms as fast as they became available. It's easy to see why she fought so hard for so long."

"But she must have known that she would not win that war," Father Matthew said softly.

"Probably, but she had to fish to live. When they came the third time and talked to her about how the dam would help irrigate the area, and attract more farmers and how dirt-poor homesteaders would be able to make a living, she listened. And then there was the vision of cheap electricity. But she didn't buy off on the argument that it was good for everyone—no one even considered the Indians. As the story goes, the Feds couldn't understand why she wouldn't want to take the money and move anyplace she wanted."

"I guess we know how Milly responded to that," Father Matthew smiled.

"'Over my dead body!' comes to mind. She didn't care about building a dam. She told the government agents it was a wrongheaded decision. It would destroy the fish and she and the Indians, and anyone else who depended on the river, would starve. Or at least I can imagine her telling them that."

"So what finally changed her mind?" asked Father Matthew.

"I think over time everything wore her down. Over and over, her sister wrote letters and told her to accept the money or the government would take the property and she would be left talking to herself. I have some of those letters."

Father Matthew leaned forward, his chin propped on his hands and repeated the argument: "Milly, that dam will be built with or without you. Save yourself."

"That's the picture of Great-aunt Milly I grew up with, a lean, hard woman who survived the early thirties, who eventually sold her property to the federal government and moved to one of those small white houses in Grand Coulee, fuming and sputtering every step of the way, forever resentful that a big dam was built on her land."

The two sleuths sat quietly on the bench by the river and breathed in the warm summer air. Finally Father Matthew asked "Do you remember how old you were when you first heard that Milly shot a priest?"

Maggie shifted to a warmer spot on the bench and said "About five or six. Everybody tuned me out. When I was finally old enough to ask my father what happened, he said he didn't know. End of conversation. I didn't believe him for a minute. Then, just before he died, he asked me to sit with him. He wanted me to know something about Milly. He never told me what it was because as he started to talk he had a massive stroke and died. I guess that's the core of my obsession. I know something happened. I just don't know what."

"Does anyone else in the family care to know what happened?"

"No, not really. This is my own personal obsession." Maggie, laughed softly. "I just can't seem to let it go. You should hear my brother Lucas whenever I bring up Milly. He rolls his eyes and groans. He thinks I should use my vacation for something fun like climbing Mt. Rainier or going to Hawaii, all things he would really like to do. As for my mother, Milly wasn't her relative, so she has no interest. Just me and my obsession."

"I guess there are worse things to be obsessed by." Father Matthew looked at the clock tower and rose from the bench. "I need to get back. Bishop Davis does not tolerate being late for prayers. Are you staying in Spokane tomorrow?"

"I am." Her answer was crisp and short. "This is taking more time than I thought it would, but this is why I'm here and I'm determined to find some answers even if I don't really know what the questions are. I'll try the Historical Society tomorrow."

Father Matthew Brannigan picked up their sandwich wrappers and held out his hand to help her off the bench. "I'm here to assist you, Maggie Callahan. Bishop's orders!" he grinned.

With that they left the river walk, each with questions, doubts, and uncertainties teeming in their heads. It had been a heady afternoon.

CHAPTER NINE

As agreed the day before, they met at River Park the next evening to compare notes. Maggie remembered to bring a warm sweater knowing the evenings cooled considerably by the river. She smiled when she saw Father Matthew. "Let's walk," he said. "I love the evening hours and I need to get some exercise."

"Fine with me." I must find out more about him, she thought, as she rose to join her long legged companion.

"I'd like to see more of the gardens. Let's head for the wooden bridge," she said, matching the priest stride for stride. Maggie, too, loved to walk, so they proceeded at a fast pace.

Only a few steps into their semi-sprint, Father Matthew said, "What did you find out at the Historical Society?"

"I found absolutely nothing. I started with Great-aunt Milly's name. Nothing surfaced. I looked under Evangeline Doyle—that was my grandmother's maiden name. Nothing except a marriage license dated 1939 when she married Daniel Callahan. Then I talked to the sheriff to see what was in their files. Nothing. I guess that's a positive, but very discouraging nonetheless. What did you do? Did you visit the archives again?"

"I sifted through the museum part of the archives. Nothing there to help you, but I did have an interesting discussion with my friend, Father Francesco. I'll tell you about it, but first tell me about your grandmother, Evangeline. She was your grandmother, right? Who was she and what was she like?"

Maggie sighed. This was going nowhere, she thought. Maybe Lucas was right. I should have taken a real vacation. Then she thought about all the priest had done for her, so she smiled because it was so easy to talk about the grandmother she'd loved so much.

"Grandmother Evangeline was a pioneer in the truest sense of the word," she began. "She came west on a train from St. Joseph, Missouri when she was very young, probably about seventeen. She wanted to teach school. She had attended a normal school in Missouri to be certified as a teacher. She also wanted adventure, so against her parents' wishes, she and a friend boarded a train to San Francisco. For whatever reason, they found their way up to the greater Spokane area, probably because that was near where Milly lived. I'm not sure she had a job waiting, but she got one and taught high school."

Their pace slowed as she talked. "When she died I found some diaries. What a treasure! It took me a year to get up nerve to read them—it felt like voyeurism, you know. Spying on my own grandmother. In one there were several entries about one of the boys who gave her a hard time—said he hated school, and was very disrespectful. So she borrowed a horse, rode out to his ranch to talk to his parents and told them that if he wanted to stay in school, he had to behave and do his schoolwork. She told them she wouldn't tolerate insolent students. The next day the father brought the boy to school, and in front of the students, told her she would never have another problem with his son. And she didn't. He became a model student. Later he became an attorney."

"Have you read all the diaries?" Father Matthew asked. "They might hold some of the answers you're looking for."

"I've read every word. I've wondered if it's a coincidence that several years are missing—the very years we're investigating."

"I suppose that could be a piece of the puzzle. What else do you know about your grandmother's early life?"

"Except for a year or so when she helped Milly settle into her place in Idaho, she lived in or around Spokane. She taught school until she married. Then she lost her job because it was not proper for a woman to be married and teach school. She might get pregnant and how would that look in front of impressionable children? Somehow carrying a child implied behavior unbecoming to a lady."

Maggie snickered at such antiquated thinking. "Where did they think all those children came from? It was that old-fashioned attitude that a woman's place is in the home, but my attitude is a woman belongs in the House and the Senate."

Father Matthew laughed and Maggie went on. "Anyway, later on, Grandmother Evangeline became something of a country doctor. I still have the doctor's manual she used. It's interesting because it contains many cures that we now consider folk medicine. It covered everything and was called *The People's Home Medical Library: Medicine for people and animals*." Maggie smiled to herself as she thought of the old musty-smelling book her family fondly called the horse doctor book. She treasured that book and all the special notations her grandmother had made in the margins like births, deaths, marriages, and special recipes to cure all manner of ailments for horses and humans. "After that she was a nurse and had a long gig as a midwife who delivered many, many babies over her lifetime."

Matthew picked it up. "Thankfully, we've become more tolerant—a woman can have a child and be in the house or the senate, or even a classroom." His eyes twinkled.

Maggie nodded, but wondered if the priest was aware the struggle for equal rights for women was still raging. She decided not to argue the point.

"Milly was older?" Father Matthew seemed to be taking a real interest in her family. His asking was more than Maggie expected. By now they had slowed down to a leisurely stroll.

"Yes, by six years. She married Ben back in St. Joseph and they moved to the coulee. She loved Ben, the coulee, the river, the Indians. It was a tragedy, losing Ben so soon." The breeze off the river began to chill the evening air. As Maggie pulled the sweater around her shoulders, she said, "The one thing I love about this area is that it can be a hundred degrees during the day, but at night it cools off enough to sleep."

"Yes, it reminds me of deserts where I've lived."

Now is my chance to learn about him, she thought. Weary of all the dead ends she'd faced in the last two days, she wanted to learn something new. "Father, what about your parents? What were they like?"

Father Matthew grinned. It was pleasant to have someone his own age interested in him as someone other than a priest. "Let's find a bench, but I have to leave soon. I'd like to enjoy the river and watch the hummingbirds drink. I'm always amazed at how much energy they expend for a little nourishment. I wasn't very old when I found out they eat mosquitoes. I was surprised to learn they needed protein. Everyone should have hummies and swallows to keep the mosquito population down." She found his interest in nature attractive.

They found a bench and sat, watching the river. "Maggie, I'd love to tell you all about my parents because I had a great life growing up under their watchful eyes, but I have to get back soon. My dad was military and my mom followed him all over the world. So there are lots of stories, but they'll have to be for another time. May I walk you back to your room?"

She was disappointed that their visit was cut short. "No, thanks. I'll take my time walking back through the park. The flow of the river relaxes me." She was ready to reflect on what they hadn't learned and to consider where to go next.

"I'll talk to you tomorrow and pray for an epiphany tonight." He shook Maggie's hand warmly, turned and walked back down the path. She watched him retrace their route along the river and looked forward to their next meeting.

CHAPTER TEN

The next day was a sizzler. Maggie walked to a diner just down the street from her rented room. Father Matthew had called early that morning and asked her to meet him for lunch. It was an old 1950s diner he particularly liked with black and white diamond tiled floors, red booths each with a juke box attached to the wall, a soda fountain, and the ambiance of saddle shoes and petticoats.

Her dad was heavy in her thoughts as she walked along. She realized that she actually knew very little about her father's early life, other than when he was fifteen his father had died of meningitis. Then only three months later his brother succumbed to it. Maggie had it too as a child. Maybe there was a genetic link.

She knew her dad left Spokane to find a job after his father died. When he was turned down for work at the dam, he just kept moving, working as a laborer doing odd jobs until he got a job cooking at the Pilot Butte Inn in Bend, Oregon. He ended up being head chef, but that was about all she knew until he and Mom met and moved to Portland, Oregon and then to Seattle. She realized she actually knew more about her great-aunt's youth than she knew about her dad's and that was disturbing to admit.

She pushed the door to the diner open and a bell rang to alert the waitress who ushered her to a booth toward the back. She only had time to scan the menu before he was in the doorway, tall and dark, wearing black jeans with a short-sleeved black shirt. And the ever-present white collar.

She raised her hand and waved to him. "Father, over here." He turned to her, smiled and in a half dozen long strides was seated across from her.

"So glad you made it. I'm starving. Have you ordered?" he asked.

"Not yet, but the tuna fish sandwich and iced tea call to me." Maggie closed the menu signaling she had made up her mind. Father Matthew agreed with her choice and they placed their order.

They settled back in the booth and Maggie, always straight to the point, started the conversation. "I know you haven't found anything in your rummaging through all those boxes and I want you to know how grateful I am for your help. But now I want to change the subject a little. I don't get to talk philosophy with clergy very often and I'm curious about where the Church stands on several issues."

"Ask your questions and I will tell you what I know." He leaned back and studied the inquiring face across the table.

"What do you know about celibacy?" Maggie asked just as the waitress appeared with the iced tea.

Father Matthew startled and sat bolt upright. The waitress slammed the glasses down and fled.

Maggie hastily took a sip of iced tea to help stifle the impulse to giggle. "Let me rephrase that."

"I would appreciate it," the priest said, sipping his own iced tea. They both managed to keep serious expressions.

"What I mean is, what can you tell me about celibacy and Church policy? I know celibacy is mandatory, but what has the Church done to control sexual abuse by priests over the years or what have they done about a priest who wants to marry?" Maggie sipped her iced tea and looked at the priest with a steady gaze.

Father Matthew held the gaze for a moment and then blinked. "You can really throw 'em in from left field, Maggie. Where are we going with this?"

"Well, I'm trying to think of reasons a woman would shoot a priest. Child abuse and celibacy, or lack thereof, are the two major reasons I can think of," she said, still looking closely at Father Matthew. "Now Milly had no children, so that kind of rules out one or at least puts it on the back burner. But priests have a history of having affairs."

Father Matthew took a deep breath and was about to begin just as a nervous looking waitress came with their tuna fish sandwiches. He waited until she was gone. "All right. Maybe a little history is in order. The church requires priests to take a vow of celibacy when they are ordained. But that hasn't always been true. Early priests were allowed to have wives. If you go back to the Middle Ages, cohabitation was not a secret and celibacy was enforced by only a few of the more ascetic and holy, devoted theologians. Later the Protestant Reformation tried to make sexual encounters of any kind outside of marriage, taboo. Then, in the mid 1500's, the Council of Trent demanded that all clergy be subject to discipline for indulging in sex of any kind. The hypocrisy in all that was that while they mandated clerical celibacy, they also recognized that a man was happier in a married relationship." He hesitated and then added, "Probably did a better job."

Maggie smiled and nodded to show her appreciation of his forthrightness, but remained silent while the priest took a bite of his sandwich.

"About the same time," he continued, "when Henry VIII was fighting for religious supremacy and freedom from the papacy, the Church tried to enforce celibacy. There were economic reasons for that. The Church did not want priests leaving their land to heirs. If priests had families and estates, the wealth was subdivided among their survivors and that diluted the value of the priests' holdings. The Church got left out. So the simple answer was to deny priests the privilege of having families who would suck money away from the Church."

"That's a new wrinkle," Maggie said through a mouthful of tuna. She swallowed and wiped her mouth with her napkin. "Now here's another side of this issue. I'm aware the Church doesn't provide you with a retirement program, so how do priests live when they get too old to work and they have no family to take care of them?"

"Aging priests are retired to seminaries or monasteries where they live out their lives. Many remain active in the Church and they're still able to perform their priestly duties. Some, such as my friend and mentor, Father Francesco, write books and position papers for and about the Church."

"Why aren't they allowed to save toward their retirement?"

"Most go in when they're teens, so they never build up any reserves. I worked for years before I entered the priesthood. I have a trust that I may not touch, but it will make me secure in my older years if I ever leave the priesthood."

Leave the priesthood? Maggie blinked but smothered a gasp and hastened to move on. "Back to business—I want to explore how the practice of priestly celibacy might have affected my great-aunt's life."

The priest frowned. "I'm not sure how to answer that, Maggie."

"Let's lay the cards on the table, Father Matthew. I wonder if Milly might have been sexually exploited by a priest. An affair gone off the skids? It's easy to believe she could have been vulnerable after she lost her husband. Charlie Williams said she was a devoted Catholic always helping Father Gregory."

"Could be, Maggie. It happens, we all know that." Father Matthew squeezed the wedge of lemon into his iced tea and looked at her, recognizing the conversation had taken another twist. "Did the gossip ever lean in that direction?"

"No, but there may have been innuendo when I was too young to pick up on it."

"Who did most of the talking at these family gatherings?"

"The aunties. My mother's sisters. No relation, they just liked to gossip. Milly was my father's mother's sister. That was the Catholic side of the family. My mother's sisters were married to evangelical ministers and these discussions seemed to be their answer to good cheer at Christmas. Nattering about Great-aunt Milly was the 'in' thing for those puritanical old biddies. I never felt they were especially Christian."

"Did anyone else ever suggest it was your great-aunt who did the shooting?"

Maggie suddenly feared that she was giving this priest information he could use to cover up what she wanted to know. Was he getting information that the bishop could use to build another barrier for her? Or did he sincerely want to help her? She decided to trust him.

"To be honest, Dad and Grandmother Evangeline gave mixed messages. They wouldn't tolerate the gossip, but they put a stop to it with things like, 'We're not going to talk about anyone shooting a priest,' rather than 'There never was a shooting.' You hear the difference?"

Matthew nodded.

"Grandmother Evangeline insisted Milly never shot a priest, but she'd say, 'Milly didn't do it,' not, 'It never happened.' So the protests never closed the door on the story, and they didn't close the door on talking about it either because the instant my father and my grandmother were out of earshot it all started again."

"So you believed the story because no one ever gave you reason to believe it didn't happen," Matthew summarized. "And the aunties made no effort to protect you from their loose talk."

"Yes. That's how I remember it." Maggie toyed with the straw in her iced tea and felt tears welling up. "Father, from childhood I was programmed to believe my great-aunt shot a priest. I've lived with the fascination and the horror of it all my life."

The tears spilled over and Maggie struggled to control herself while Father Matthew looked on with compassion in his eyes. He leaned across the table and looked at her until their eyes locked.

"Maggie, you were a victim of a subtle form of child abuse. Can you understand that?"

"I can now, Father. But I must find out what really happened—the truth. Can you understand that?"

"I can now, Maggie."

They sat in silence until Maggie's emotions were calmed and Father Matthew resumed the conversation. "You know, the theory about an assignation gone awry is plausible, but the fact remains we don't have a corpse. You say Father Gregory lives in Texas, and no priests seem to have gotten themselves shot between 1930 and 1939. Not around here, anyway."

"But we haven't given up, have we?" she asked.

"Well I haven't. Have you?" Father Matthew laughed. "Uh-oh! Time flies when the conversation is so rich with mystery, but I'm afraid I must be off." He called for the check and began to slide toward the edge of the booth.

"Before you go, Father, can I ask one last question? Why did you enter the priesthood?"

Father Matthew Brannigan looked bewildered by the question. "Why do you ask?"

"You've been very kind to me. It's such a contrast from Bishop Davis and, frankly, any priest I've ever known. They've all been so," she searched for the right word, "distant."

Father Matthew settled back down. Maybe he didn't have to be back just yet. "I'm basically just a nice guy." Father Matthew grinned, then switched the subject to Maggie. "Tell me, what kind of job do you have?"

"I'm a journalist—I cover natural disasters. And I love my job."

She could see his surprise. "Well, not the disaster part, of course. But I'm usually the first one asked to go into a disaster area. I study it and collect data that might help them deal with, or even prevent the next one. Then I write articles for my company and more often than not they get published. I like those bylines," she grinned.

"But isn't it dangerous?"

"Sometimes, but I've had lots of training. I don't mind saying I know my way around a disaster,"

"Now you're bragging," he laughed. "With all the disasters running rampant around the world, how can you take time for this side trip?"

"This is called my summer vacation. Pathetic, huh?"

"Not pathetic at all. You're on a mission," Father Matthew mused. "Your work sounds interesting. Any down sides, other than being in mortal danger?"

"Just one—the guy I work with." Maggie rolled her eyes. "I'd like to take him for a long walk off a short pier."

"I want to hear more, but it'll have to be later or I'll be late for my meeting with the bishop. It's not healthy to keep the bishop waiting." With that he paid the check and was out the door.

Once again Maggie watched the priest walk away. It had been so easy to talk to him. She felt safe. With a start, she realized she had let him pay for her lunch. She would have to remember to thank him.

CHAPTER ELEVEN

Bishop Davis sat at his desk, the Meerschaum nowhere to be seen. "Come in. Sit," he demanded, his tone gruff. "Well, what have you learned about Miss Callahan?"

Father Matthew sat in the chair facing the desk. "Not much, sir. She talked mostly about her family and her job, not much about the search." He had no intention of telling the bishop about her questions on celibacy.

"I suppose she's determined to continue this cockamamie investigation of hers," he said, signaling his disgust with Maggie Callahan and her infernal snooping.

"Yes sir, I believe she is. She is a very determined young woman." Father Matthew wondered what it was about Maggie that annoyed the bishop.

Bishop Davis set his jaw and pondered that for a moment. "Hmm. Very well. Thank you. You are dismissed, Father Brannigan."

Father Matthew rose, dutifully dropped his head slightly, and walked toward the door. The bishop was set on being a road block for Maggie as she reached out to him for help. Where was kindness?

Benevolence? Consideration? This didn't feel like what he signed up for when he took his final vows.

"One more thing, Father Matthew. Forget about those iron doors. There is nothing in there that pertains to her search."

"Of course there is," Father Matthew muttered under his breath, his jaw set in annoyance at this latest encounter with his superior. It was going to be a long assignment in this diocese. "Yes sir, I understand," he said loud enough to be heard.

CHAPTER TWELVE

"Bless me, Father, I want to sin." Father Matthew grinned at his old friend and mentor. Father Francesco held out his hands in greeting. The rotund priest, his ruddy round face covered with age spots and sun baked wrinkles, was warm and welcoming. He had guided Matthew through his years in the seminary and had been there for him ever since his ordination.

"Do enter before Satan tempts you further, my son. Even though I am not your confessor, I will listen to the nature of your misery." Father Francesco smiled as he made the sign of the cross, blessing his young friend.

Father Matthew entered Father Francesco's modest cottage and scooped the old man up in a hug that spoke of their deep friendship. The room was a sweltering 85 degrees, the required thermal units it took to warm the arthritic joints of an old man. Books and papers stacked in uneven piles lined the floor. Narrow paths led to the bedroom and kitchen. It was amazing the aging priest could find his way through the debris. Father Francesco would always say he had too much to read and think about and wanted it all close at hand. He was noted for his puckish sense of humor and renowned for his speaking skills and his ability to recruit new priests. He was regularly sent to seminaries to find the best potential priests then guide them through the first years of their priesthood. He considered Father Matthew one of the most gifted and capable young priests he had ever mentored.

Father Matthew released his friend and said, "My misery is Bishop Davis."

Father Francesco sighed with full understanding. "I don't see Hail Marys or a novena working for this misery, my friend. What's the problem? Wait. Don't tell me until I get us a cup of tea." He moved in the direction of the kitchen.

Matthew cleared a stack of newspapers and pamphlets from a side chair and settled in for a chat over hot tea in a hot room on a hot day.

Father Francesco shuffled back, balancing the teacups on a tray. "Does your need for atonement have anything to do with Miss Callahan?" he asked, knowing full well that it did. "How is the quest coming along?"

Father Matthew told him about the bishop's obstructionist attitude. "Bishop Davis asked me to do the searches and then he puts up road blocks. He insists that I only examine the records for specific years and he won't allow me access to that iron door I told you about."

Father Francesco did not respond immediately so Matthew went on. "I found a similar door off the archives at my church and Bishop Davis won't allow me to enter that room either. I get a sense that whatever we are looking for must be behind one of those doors." He paused for a sip of tea.

Father Francesco said flatly, "I do know about the iron doors, but I can't get you through either one of them. The rooms are off limits to everyone but the bishop or his designee, in order to file documents."

Matthew blurted out, "What is the church hiding? Are there skeletons buried behind those doors?"

Father Francesco riveted the young priest with his gaze. "Why are you so passionate about this search, Matthew?"

Father Matthew sat back in his chair, bewildered by his friend's question. "In the beginning I did it because it was a reasonable request and I was told to do it by the bishop, but now I think something is being hidden from Miss Callahan. Gut feeling, you know." He stopped abruptly and squared his shoulders. "I'm sorry I came to you with this, Father. The last thing I want to do is put you in a compromising position with the bishop. Please forgive me."

"There is nothing to forgive," Father Francesco said gently. The calm, reassuring hazel eyes offered the support and understanding Matthew came for.

Father Matthew toyed with his teacup, then broke the stillness with a new topic. "What is this new treatise you are working on?"

"Celibacy, and I would like your input as I develop the paper."

Father Matthew choked, remembering his discussion with Maggie. Recovering, he said, "We should invite Maggie to join one of our conversations. The topic of celibacy seems to intrigue her."

"Anything to do with you?" Father Francesco teased.

Father Matthew blushed. "I hardly think so, Father. She seems to think it might somehow be related to what happened with her great-aunt."

"Well, bring the young lady along so I can meet her. Perhaps she can provide a woman's insight on the subject." The old priest smiled and raised his cup. "I'm anxious to meet the person who has you so fired up about Church secrets. I'm sorry I cannot find you a way through the iron doors, but perhaps I can lead you and Miss Callahan in another direction."

At last, a breakthrough, Father Matthew thought, and he leaned forward to hear the old priest's words.

"Tell her go back to the newspaper and closely examine the vital statistics and the obituaries, not just the news stories. If something rings a bell, it will give you a reason to ask the bishop for a more thorough search, perhaps behind those iron doors."

Father Matthew's face did not betray the disappointment he felt. He was certain his good friend knew something that would unlock more than those iron doors. But why the secrecy? Was it information he'd obtained through a confession? "Thank you Father. I must tell you I find it troubling that Maggie feels the Church is letting her down."

Father Francesco lowered his head and nodded. "Yes, my son, that is troubling."

The young priest gave Father Francesco time to say more, but silence lay between them, opening a tiny, hurtful chasm. Finally Father Matthew stood. "I'll tell her what you said about the vital statistics." He weaved his way through the stacks of books and newspapers toward the door, then remembered he had a cup and saucer in his hands.

"I guess I shouldn't swipe your fine china, Father." They both laughed and Father Matthew went to the kitchen to rinse his dishes. On his way out he stopped to grasp his old friend's hand one more time. "I'll see you soon, Father. I'll bring Maggie by next time."

"Please do that. I look forward to meeting her and hearing what she has to say."

And once again, Father Matthew was heading back to the church even though his thoughts were heading elsewhere.

CHAPTER TWELVE

It was late afternoon when Father Matthew found Maggie in the Spokesman-Review archives looking through microfiche. Her hair hung in front of her face, like that of a red headed Labradoodle. He stood near her for a few seconds, thinking about Father Francesco's advice. Finally, he touched her shoulder to let her know he was there. She jumped, then smiled up at him.

"Didn't mean to startle you. I went to see my old friend and mentor, Father Francesco, but I had no luck with him on accessing the inner sanctum. He gave me the same run-around the bishop gave me about the iron doors."

Maggie sighed, "Just another dead end."

"But he'll help however he can. And it's your lucky day. He wants your insight on celibacy." Father Matthew laughed at Maggie's astonishment. "Oh, and he did say you should pay attention to the obits and vital statistics in these old newspapers."

Maggie's eyes widened with interest. "Vital statistics? Did he give a reason?"

Father Matthew sat on the chair at the adjoining carrel and said, "Not really. He said something might ring a bell."

Maggie frowned and rubbed her eyes. "I guess that means starting all over. I've concentrated on news and obituaries, but just skimmed over the vital stats. Sometimes they're just stuck in as fillers."

Maggie stood up and stretched. "I can't face any more microfiche today. I'll follow up on his suggestion tomorrow."

"I'll help you after morning Mass if you like," Father Matthew volunteered.

Maggie heard sincerity in his offer. "I can't tell you how much I would appreciate that," she said. "I'll be here when they open, at ten."

She turned off the microfiche reader, picked up her notebooks, put them in her bag and turned to Father Matthew. "It's the first time I've felt like I'm not in this, uh, by myself." Her voice broke and she turned away before he could see the tears spring to her eyes.

"I'll see you here at ten," he said.

Maggie picked up her bag, slung it over her shoulder, and the two walked out the door into Eastern Washington's August.

CHAPTER THIRTEEN

Later that evening Father Matthew walked back to the old priest's cottage, tapped on the door and pushed it open.

"Father?" he called to his friend.

"I'm in the kitchen," Father Francesco hollered over his shoulder. "I knew you'd be back. I'm making us another cup of tea, or I could make us a toddy. Did you deliver my message to the young lady?"

Matthew found his chair still free of clutter and settled in. "No toddy for me, and I did deliver your message, but neither of us gets the riddle and I'm becoming as disillusioned as she is."

"What? Losing faith already?" The old priest chuckled as he brought in the tea tray. "You are too young to question the authority of the Church."

"Father, I don't think I'm too young for anything anymore. I became a priest two years ago at the ripe old age of thirty-two. As you are well aware, I worked in the oil fields for eight years. When I entered the seminary I was sure it was the right decision for me, but my years in the secular world left me skeptical about some of the Church ideology."

Father Francesco relished the verbal exchanges he had with his perceptive young colleague. "Like, perhaps celibacy? Let's talk about this. I need fuel for my paper."

Father Matthew launched into the discussion with enthusiasm. "Present day Church doctrine on celibacy is hypocritical, dated, and out of touch with the real world."

"Matthew, my boy, don't be afraid to tell me how you really feel about this," Father Francesco's hearty laughter barely interrupted the young priest's attack.

"There are married priests, mostly in other countries, especially South America. There are priests who live with women. There are priests who have secret lovers. There are nuns who have strayed. I read about the murder of a pregnant nun. The killer was a priest."

He was on a roll. "And what about the Church covering up pedophilia? All I'm saying is that sex gets in the way of many true believers." Father Matthew settled into his uncomfortable chair.

Father Francesco rubbed his hands together anticipating a lively discussion and leaped into it with unbounded enthusiasm. "I agree with you. To enforce celibacy because of the manifestations of sex perhaps taints the priesthood. I can't think of anything we do that can't be done by a married priest, but celibacy is deeply ingrained into the core values and memory of the Church and it is not without merit as a virtue."

Father Matthew broke in. "We heal the sick and comfort the forlorn. We care for those forsaken and abandoned. Some of us even scale the slippery walls of the Church hierarchy. We preach the Gospel while speaking of modern day problems that are not necessarily compatible. We give communion. We marry people. We bury people. We anoint the sick and bless the dying. We teach in our schools and universities. Some of us move to higher levels in the church. We know ministers of other faiths perform all these functions while married."

"And you think the Catholic Church should also allow this?" Father Francesco's face was flushed with enjoyment.

"I do. Definitely. Why would we think Catholic men are less competent than their peers who have families and do the bidding of their churches?" He paused and studied his empty cup. "If the business of celibacy is all so arbitrary and fluid, then the Church position should be able to change again. The doctrine seems to follow with what's expedient at the time. Maybe now it's expedient to bend enough to allow both priests *and* nuns to marry."

Having made the point he carried in his heart, the young priest drew a deep breath. "May I pour more tea, Father?"

"Of course!" Father Francesco laughed heartily. Father Matthew went to the kitchen and brought the teapot back. He filled each cup and reclaimed his seat.

Father Francesco leaned forward and resumed the discussion. "Currently the Church's view is that a priest and nun must not have other family commitments. Service to God, through the Church, is the only commitment people of the cloth have time for." Father Francesco sat back and sipped his tea. "When a novitiate takes her final vows to become a nun she accepts a ring and considers herself married to God."

Father Matthew's eyes narrowed, revealing his conflict with the notion. "This only tells me the Church is unable to live in the twentieth century. Denying priests and nuns the sacrament of marriage and denying birth control when there are six billion people living on the planet is simply wrongheaded. It denies the fact that in many Catholic and non-Catholic countries, people are starving because they have children they cannot feed. And the Church continues to preach abstinence as the only accepted form of birth control. We all know how well that works."

"Good point," Father Francesco nodded. "I am not in total agreement, but willing to listen."

Father Matthew pressed on. "So many priests who have been truly celibate all of their adult lives have no connection to the needs of their parishioners. Some understand, but many women have to search for a priest that will condone birth control. What a terrible burden the church forces on women and compassionate priests. And, while I'm at it, the church says abortion is murder. If we don't want our women aborting babies, best we condone contraception."

"Another very good argument. I'm still listening."

Father Matthew continued. "And while I'm on a roll, celibacy enforces loneliness. Unless a priest is very charismatic and is frequently invited into homes on social occasions, he lives an isolated and lonely life. Some few have lives outside the ministry, but it takes someone who is totally self-contained. An example would be Father Greeley who writes romance novels. People love him and his books. And there's a nun from Italy who sings rock songs. But they're exceptional, like you. Others become bitter, especially as they age and realize they have nowhere to go and begin to wonder why they didn't make other choices. I've known a few who feel abandoned when they're forced into retirement in an old, decaying monastery. These all appear to me to be good reasons for reconsidering celibacy as Church policy."

Father Francesco looked directly at his young friend. "Did you think this through before you became a priest or are you just now coming to this line of reasoning?" Father Francesco tugged at his sleeve. "Would you leave the Church if the right person came along?"

Matthew studied his empty cup as the older priest quietly awaited his answer.

"I knew what I was doing when I became a priest. If I met someone with whom I wanted another life, I would consider it for a long time. I would not hide the relationship from the Church, but I would remain celibate until I was released from my vows."

Father Francesco paused for the briefest moment, his eyes not leaving the face of his young friend. Slowly he lifted the teapot.

"Good," he pronounced. "More tea?"

"No, thanks. Three's my limit. But I do have more to say, Father. I think there is one more problem with celibacy, the thing that should bring the Church into the real world. I suspect celibacy is the single most significant deterrent to young men becoming priests."

"Yes," Father Francesco nodded his agreement. "The Church is definitely suffering from a lack of young men wanting to become priests."

Father Matthew stood up. "That should give you plenty of material for your paper." He chuckled, knowing his wise old mentor had not heard anything he hadn't already studied in depth. But sometimes truths are buried in layers of scholarship and it takes a fresh perspective to recognize them.

"I must go, Father. I have to be up early for prayers. I hope we can continue this discussion soon."

"We will. Bring the young woman next time. We'll see how she handles herself on the subject of celibacy." The old man smiled contentedly. It had been a very good day.

CHAPTER FOURTEEN

Maggie woke early. She washed her hair and ironed a new cotton blouse. She dreaded going to read microfiche again. She figured she'd be sway-backed and permanently cross-eyed before she finished the job. But at least her misery would have company today, and because of that she took a little extra time with her grooming.

It was cool for an August morning, a good time for walking, so she took the long route to the library in order to take in the exquisite rose garden she had found behind a dilapidated picket fence. The pleasant delay tactic paid off in a feast of fragrances as she leaned over the fence to meet each bush she could reach. The rest of the yard was a muddle of dry weeds and long grass, but the roses were perfectly tended. She smiled. This gardener has priorities, she thought. Her route took her by a coffee shop tucked into a front corner of a quaint Victorian home. "Danish every morning, while they last," announced a fading sign in the window. She climbed the sun-blistered steps and bought two coffees and two cheese Danish.

Father Matthew had said he would join her at ten, but he didn't arrive until eleven, again dressed in black, but this time with no collar. By then she had consumed both Danishes. Maggie handed him the cold coffee.

"Hi, Father. I bought a sweet roll for you too, but I ate it myself. Sorry."

"I'm the one who's sorry," he said, "for being late but mostly for missing the sweet roll. What was it?"

"Cheese Danish, baked fresh this morning."

Father Matthew grimaced and shook his head. "Not cheese Danish, my favorite! That's the last time I'll ask the bishop if there's anything I can do for him when I'm due for a date with you."

"So what did His Excellence have you doing this morning?"

"Running errands which would have taken five minutes if I'd had my own car here. The Town and Country is too expensive to use for short hauls, he says. He has a warped sense of frugality, but I enjoyed the exercise. Of course I didn't know I was missing out on cheese Danish." Father Matthew wrinkled his nose at the cold coffee, but took a sip anyway. "How's it going here?" he asked.

"Slowly. I'm already brain dead." She stretched and broke into a wide smile at having a collaborator in her detective efforts. "How did the meeting go with Father Francesco? Did you learn anything we can use?"

Father Matthew sat at the carrel next to Maggie. "Nothing beyond what I already told you about looking at obituaries and vital statistics. We did have a lively discussion about celibacy."

Maggie rolled her eyes upward. "That doesn't get me any closer to solving my confounded mystery. Nothing about the key?"

"I think the only way I'll get behind that door is if I figure out a way to blast through iron. I learned a lot about dynamite when I was in the oil fields." He flashed a grin toward Maggie who responded by rolling her eyes again.

"There has to be something in there the bishop and maybe even Father Francesco doesn't want me to see," she said.

The priest nodded. "I agree about the bishop. But I'm pretty sure Father Francesco wants to help, and that leads me to believe what he won't tell us is tied to a confession." He swirled the cold coffee around in the bottom of the cup and went on. "So I guess we're back to obits and vital statistics. By the way, you're invited to join the next discussion. He would like to hear a woman's point of view on celibacy." He glanced at Maggie to see if that sparked any interest.

It did. Her eyes widened. "I'll be out of my league, but I always like a good discussion." Turning to the microfiche reader, Maggie asked Father Matthew to run name recognition for Mildred Miller and Evangeline Doyle from 1925 to 1935 and let her know what came up. It was backtracking, but fresh eyes might turn up new information. They divided up the piles of microfiche rolls. "I'll stick with the vital statistics—I'm about halfway through."

Two hours later the only thing new that had surfaced was a piece praising Evangeline Doyle for her excellent teaching. The superintendent was quoted as saying, "The position Miss Doyle vacates will be much sought-after."

"Baloney," Maggie snorted. "If the job was so great, then why did she leave?"

Father Matthew looked puzzled. "Why *did* she leave?"

"How should I know?" Maggie snapped and then exhaled loudly. "Father, I need to get out of here. I've been sitting too long. How about a hike up the hills above Minnehaha Park?"

"Best idea I've heard all day! I haven't been there yet."

Maggie's temperament visibly improved as she set about leaving. "That's where I played when we came summers to visit Grandmother Callahan. That was Evangeline, you know. The park was two blocks from her house."

They walked back to her room to get her car and stopped for a sandwich along the way. Maggie's vexation dissolved in the afternoon sun and their easy conversation covered a wide range of topics, from favorite teachers to how to stay cool in temperatures above 120 degrees, a subject on which Father Matthew claimed superior knowledge.

CHAPTER FIFTEEN

Maggie drove the four miles out of town to the trailhead. "What will the bishop think about your riding with me? Will he raise his eyebrows and look aghast—emphasis on aghast?" She smiled at Father Matthew, a twinkle in her eyes.

Father Matthew grinned in assent. "Aghast is probably a good word if he ever finds out I went walking in the hills with you, which he won't. His only question will be 'What did Miss Callahan learn from today's trip to the newspaper?' He's as obsessed about what you find as you are."

They arrived at the base of the hill and parked near the footpath. "I love these rocks," Maggie said, pointing up the hill. "Lucas and I used to play up here when we were little. We'd hunt for fossils. We never found a single fossil until we went over to the St. Joe River to visit Milly. Over there we'd find lots of them in the road cuts. I wish I'd saved them."

Father Matthew bent down to tighten a shoe lace in preparation for the climb. He didn't feel properly dressed for hiking, but he wasn't about to miss this opportunity. Walking and talking was more comfortable than asking questions face to face so he said. "Where was your grandmother's house? You said she lived nearby?"

"Back where we turned into the park there used to be a big field. She lived there. She had a huge garden and raised chickens. We always had eggs, fried, boiled, or in an omelet, for breakfast. I loved coming here. The field is gone now, replaced by lots of homes."

"So she left her teaching position and must have gone someplace else before she came back to Spokane to settle down. Where did she go?"

"You know, I'm not sure. I just know she married Grandfather Callahan and lived here in Spokane." Maggie pondered the question in her mind and searched her memory, unsuccessfully, for an answer.

They walked in silence until she asked, "Where did you grow up? You said you would tell me about your family when you didn't have to hurry back to your real job with the church."

"I guess I did say something like that. I grew up all over the world as a military brat. I've lived in Japan, France, Italy, Morocco and Jordan. As a kid I picked up languages by just playing with local kids. After college, before I entered the seminary, I worked for an oil company in Iraq. I speak several languages moderately well—French, Italian, some Spanish, limited Japanese, but plenty of Arabic and Farsi." He smiled. "I had no trouble getting a job."

Maggie's eyes went wide in admiration. "Wow! I'm impressed. Would you like to work overseas again?"

"Yes, if the situation was right. I've thought about applying for work in a parish somewhere in South America, or Australia or New Zealand, but in my line of work I go where they send me and that's that."

They were now at the high point in the rocks where they stopped to look at the panoramic view of old valley houses. Maggie spread her arms in a far-reaching arc. "We'd play up here for hours, then we'd go down to the field and try to catch mice. Mother appreciated the fact that we rarely caught any. We climbed trees and tried to catch crows because we heard we could teach them to talk. Never got one. We made slingshots and shot at rabbits. Never hit one. We didn't have a lot of successes, but we sure had fun and we always slept well after all that playing."

"The mouse thing seems like an odd game to play."

"When you have energy to expend and nobody around to tell you what to do, chasing field mice makes perfect sense."

Once back on the trail Matthew asked, noting how happy Maggie sounded recalling the time she spent here as a child, "Do you consider Spokane your home?"

"Not really. I was born here, but we left when I was a baby. Seattle is home now. I went to Seattle University, you know." She turned and looked at Father Matthew to see if he registered any reaction that she had gone to a Jesuit university. Perhaps a twitch of an eyebrow. "Do you have any place you call home, Father? Living all over the world gives you a global perspective, but it doesn't sink any roots."

"I made a lot of friends everywhere I lived, right up until I hit Iraq. There I came up against a closed society. People who work in the oil fields aren't close. It's just a job. It's one of the reasons I left." He smiled, looked at Maggie and added, "I'm a people person, an extrovert you know."

"Is that why you became a priest?" She was relentless in trying to learn what made this man tick.

"Maybe part of the reason. My parents always made sure the Catholic Church was part of our lives no matter where we lived. In every country they found spiritual retreats for me to attend. Most of my close friends also attended Catholic schools. Spirituality was never available to me in Iraq. If I'd wanted to convert to Islam, I could have found many ways to study. I did a lot of reading of the religion, but it never quite clicked with me. My passion was with the Catholic Church."

Maggie was quiet for a while, and then she found the courage to tell him her conflicted feelings about the Church she both loved and hated. "You probably won't like what I am going to say, but I find the Catholic Church to be a closed society. It's patriarchal and the process for inclusion isn't very inviting. Making someone attend classes for six months in order to be accepted doesn't really invite newcomers, does it? I've known many people who have been deeply hurt by 'The Church.'" With two fingers on each hand, she formed quotation marks around the "The Church."

"Are you anti-religion or just leery of the Catholic Church?" he asked, genuinely curious about where this young woman stood on religion.

"Neither. I just hate anything that smacks of exclusion. A Lutheran pastor I know baptized a homeless man who was trying to get his life together—no strings attached, no big long confirmation class. I don't think that would happen in the Holy Names Cathedral. Honestly, I wish there was a way for people to enjoy spirituality without an organized religion telling them what to do and what to think."

"Have you studied Buddhism? Maybe it would be a better philosophical fit for you. I think you're saying that you want the conscious mind to believe in faith, but without restrictions. Sort of a meditation that anyone can do on their own."

"Maybe," Maggie said. I know a woman who followed a guru because she believed in what it brings to faith.

This was his opening to explain his own belief system. "For me, daily prayer is a form of meditation. It's my link to my conscience, my way of defining right from wrong, good over evil. During morning prayers I pray that I'll be compassionate and wise in all my encounters during the day and in the evening I pray that I was helpful in guiding people to make wise choices. The process strengthens my own faith."

She lowered her eyes as she contemplated this information and noticed how dusty his typically shiny black shoes had become on the trail. How easy it was to become distracted when she was with this man. She forced her attention back to the conversation. "Father, would you say that faith is belief?" she asked.

"Yes. To have faith is to believe and trust. It is the certainty that something is true. Faith is the cornerstone of religion. People have faith because they believe that what is said is the direct word of God and God cannot lie."

"Then why do people tear each other apart in the name of faith? That doesn't fit the basic precepts of any religion I know about." Maggie walked, shifting her gaze from Father Matthew to the narrow dirt path. "I'd like a faith that leads the human race to build better lives. I think that's what church should be about."

"You don't think that's happening?"

"I think sometimes, maybe. But it depends so much on leadership. In the case of the Church, who is the leader? The pope or the local priests? I opt for the local priests. I think they carry the burden of reason and faith. They're the ones who create a place where people want to come together and learn and build community and trust and all that leads to faith."

Maggie knew she was rambling so she stopped talking and motioned to a small stone building they were approaching on the left, an old rock shelter, no door and open holes where windows used to be. They peered inside to see two benches and a table carved with initials.

"This used to be one of my favorite places when I was a kid." She laughed. "I swear, I think that's the same blocky old furniture my brother and I played on."

They stepped inside, out of the sun, and Maggie felt a chill. She backed out of the enclosure. Father Matthew followed her and they proceeded along the trail.

"Can you hear the wind shake the long pine needles? The smell of pine should be a bottled fragrance. It speaks of long walks in the woods and is the perfume of my childhood, right here on this hillside." Thoughts of her childhood gave way to a new idea.

"Let's head over to the falls," she said brightly. "It's a breathtaking sight. Below the falls the river flows through an incredible canyon."

"Sounds like fun," he said. Their talk of faith was over.

With mischief in her eyes, Maggie said, "We could rent a kayak and forget to tell Bishop Davis you were running the river with a woman not your sister. But you'd have to wear a life vest, just in case you needed to be saved," Maggie teased. She was pretty sure Father Matthew Brannigan would not need to be saved, in or out of the water.

"Now you're mocking me again, Miss Callahan. That is disrespectful of my very white collar, which I'm not wearing today." He could give it as well as take it.

They lingered at the overlook, soaking up the beauty of the falls and marveling at the awesome power of water gushing through cataracts in the rocks, each relishing the opportunity to banter with a friend in such a place.

At last, Matthew said, "It's hard to break away from this, but I have to get back to town. By the time we walk out and drive back, it'll be time for prayers." The magic of the moment was fading and they turned back to the trail. Shortly he said, "By the way, when would you like to meet Father Francesco?"

"Any time. I'd love to meet your friend. But there must be dozens of women in this parish he can talk to. Why me?" Maggie was direct.

"Because I told him you could hold your own in an argument about celibacy." Father Matthew looked to see if there was a reaction. There wasn't.

"I suspect he won't like what I have to say."

"You might be surprised. He's a very open-minded priest."

With that, they left behind one of the best afternoons either of them had enjoyed in a very long time.

CHAPTER SIXTEEN

Father Francesco scurried down the dark stairs leading to the archives. His body was not up to the challenge of moving so quickly, but he felt he must hurry through this most unusual assignment. His chin was tucked against his chest, his shoulders tense as he went about his mission. Clutching the keys the bishop had thrust in his hand, he approached the iron door. It creaked open after he carefully turned the key in the lock. He had to use his entire body weight to pull it open enough to enter. He reached for the light switch and smiled to himself, thinking that Father Matthew had guessed correctly. This room held many secrets.

He carefully removed a box marked 1936 and carried it to a small table located under the only light in the windowless room. He shuffled through the contents until his eye caught a date on a green file folder. He carefully removed two documents briefly skimmed them, and shoved one into the pocket of his flowing robe. He removed the green folder and returned the box to its place on the shelf. He pulled the box marked 1940 from its place on the shelf and stuffed the green folder with its remaining document into the middle of the crowded box. Then he exited and locked the iron door behind him. Once outside the room, he kissed his cross, crossed himself again, and slowly ascended the stairs on legs that struggled against gravity. He huffed and puffed and gasped for air, grumbling about what all those birthdays had done to his body.

The old priest contemplated what he would say to the bishop and how he would let Father Matthew know what he had in his possession. With the bishop, he would use his most professional demeanor. With Matthew, he didn't know. With luck there would be no need to let even a hint of what he'd retrieved escape his lips. He would find another way.

He hesitated at the bishop's office door where he again crossed himself before he tapped lightly, then slowly entered the bishop's realm.

"Ah, there you are. Did you find the papers?" The bishop did not invite him to sit down, so Father Francesco rocked back and forth from one foot to the other trying to alleviate the anxiety and the nagging arthritic ache in his heels.

"I did."

"And you removed them, as I requested?"

"I did." Father Francesco's heart pounded for fear the bishop would ask to see them—both of them.

"You will hide them, as I requested, away from prying eyes?" the bishop thundered.

"I will."

Bishop Davis looked down at his paperwork. "Just give me my keys and go, but put those papers safely out of sight."

"I understand, Eminence." Father Francesco exhaled a long breath and handed the bishop the keys, but kept one in his pocket, hoping the bishop wouldn't notice. He let himself out the door. In the hall he sighed and crossed himself again. He looked at the saints' pictures hanging on the walls. He could feel their eyes on him, staring back. He wondered how judgmental they were. I really don't understand what I'm doing, he thought. Making the sign of the cross over and over as he returned to his cottage, he muttered out loud, "Of course I understand. Show me the way, Lord."

CHAPTER SEVENTEEN

There was no sun when Father Matthew woke. A grey day east of the Cascade Mountains seldom occurred during the summer, so people tended to rush outside to do things under a cool sky. It was a perfect day to visit Father Francesco. Maybe it wouldn't be stifling hot in his cottage. After morning prayers he called Maggie to see if she wanted to join them. "I can meet you outside the chapel," he said, his voice eager.

Maggie accepted the offer with enthusiasm. She was excited to meet the priest who was writing a treatise on celibacy, although she couldn't imagine that his position would vary much from the church's official position.

Father Matthew was waiting in his black pants and shirt, this time with a starched white collar. As they walked past the gardens, he said, "Smell that honeysuckle! It must have followed us here." He pointed and said, "Hang a left here. Father Francesco's cottage is out behind the school."

When they arrived Maggie was surprised to see a much older priest than she was expecting, perhaps in his late seventies or early eighties. He was shorter than Maggie and on the plump side. Impish gray eyes revealed a keen mind. Everything about him from his welcoming smile to the double chin that shook when he spoke made her want to know him better. She easily understood Matthew's fondness for the elderly priest

"Father Francesco, may I introduce Miss Maggie Callahan." Father Matthew gently nudged Maggie forward.

Maggie extended her hand. Father Francesco grabbed both her hands in his own callous-free hands and squeezed them gently. He looked up at her said, "Ah, it's the Maggie Callahan I've been waiting to meet. So good of you to come and share a cloudy morning with an old man."

"It's my pleasure, Father." Maggie didn't know whether she should pull her hands away, but after a few seconds, Father Francesco let go and motioned her to a chair. "I've been looking forward to meeting you, Father Francesco. Father Matthew speaks so highly of you,"

The old priest laughed. "Huh. That's just one Jesuit speaking of another. If I were a Benedictine, he probably wouldn't say such nice things." Maggie couldn't help but grin. She felt her anxiety melt away and accepted his invitation to sit. She sank into the chair that had been hastily cleared of magazines and newspapers.

"Father Matthew tells me you write policy papers for the Vatican. Does that mean you write policy papers that are accepted by the pope?"

Father Francesco shook his head, "Goodness no. I am one of hundreds that present the American point of view, my dear, a viewpoint that is often in opposition to Vatican interpretation of a given subject. I send my paper to a committee and if they like it, then I talk with the head of the committee. I may have to rewrite as many as a dozen times. Then if I'm lucky, it may go to the pope and I may go to the Vatican to defend my point of view. I have a pretty good track record, but there are no guarantees that my thoughts will make it past the initial review committee."

"What a responsibility," Maggie exclaimed, "to speak for American Catholics, especially when your position may differ from the Vatican hierarchy."

"I'm not always good at keeping my mouth shut. Often I think they're wrong, but I'm caught in the position of having to placate them in order to get my paper past them. It's my struggle and I find I have to compromise on occasion, much as I might not want to." In the same breath he turned his focus to his current effort. "I believe Father Matthew told you I am working on a paper regarding celibacy."

Maggie marveled at how easily he cut through the small talk and went straight to the heart of the topic at hand. "He did and I'm interested to hear what you have to say."

Father Francesco settled a little deeper in his chair, delighted at the opportunity to have a philosophical exchange with a laywoman. "Well, we know it's a divisive subject that silently splits the Church. One of the primary purposes of this paper is to stimulate open discussion. The more conservative wing of the Church wants to maintain celibacy as a fundamental tenet for all orders within the Church, while more progressive clerics lean toward a new line of thinking. They want the right to marry and have children."

Maggie nodded in assent. "I suppose the first hurdle is to get both sides into a conversation." Father Matthew looked on obviously intrigued by how this discussion was evolving.

Father Francesco was ready for a battle. "There is history to overcome, but there is also a need to look at celibacy as an old rite that no longer applies to present day needs. Besides, there is nothing written that ever suggested Jesus was celibate or that he ever told his disciples they must remain celibate. The first pope, Peter, was a married man. Most of the apostles were married and some scholars suggest Jesus was married to Mary Magdalene. The Russian Orthodox Church allows marriage and they are in good standing with the Vatican. But Russian Orthodox policy is a topic for another time. You and I must talk further on these subjects. Father Matthew is helping me with my thoughts, and I am interested in your perspective as well."

"I'm honored, Father. My perspective can be summed up pretty simply: the Church needs to cut its antiquated ties to history and meet its followers in today's world."

"Well said, daughter!" Father Francesco clapped his hands and fairly quivered in anticipation. "A brilliant opening salvo. But perhaps we should table the debate until we've had some tea and a chance to discuss your reasons for being here in Spokane."

"I'll get it, Father." Father Matthew went into the tiny kitchen and put the tea kettle on the stove.

"The cups are in the cupboard above the stove," Father Francesco called out. "Use the company porcelain." Out of sight of Father Francesco, Matthew rolled his eyes. The instructions were hardly necessary. He had poured tea hundreds of times, but not usually in the company porcelain, he had to admit.

Rummaging around in the high cupboard for the right cups, Father Matthew saw a manila envelope stuffed behind the porcelain cups, a strange place to store paperwork. "1936" was written on the outside, so he pulled it out and peered at the document inside, which appeared to be a letter. But he didn't take it out as it would be bad manners to intrude on Father Francesco's privacy.

"Do you need some help?" Father Francesco called from the living room. Father Matthew quickly replaced the envelope.

"It's fine. I'll be right in."

He poured the boiling water, noticeably distracted as he darted glances at the envelope in the cupboard. The obvious question was whether it had anything to do with Maggie's search. The obvious answer was to come back later and ask Father Francesco.

When Father Matthew returned with the tea tray and handed out the cups, the two were chatting amicably, Maggie facing Father Francesco. She was explaining the story of her now-familiar family lore. "So I'm trying to find out first if it really happened, and if so, why did it happen and was my aunt involved."

"That's a tall order. What have you found thus far?"

"I'm speculating that something happened because I've heard the story since I was little, and it has never wavered. But now I'm pretty sure it did not happen at Grand Coulee. If it happened here, in Spokane, I'm still looking for clues but nothing is popping up. It's frustrating, to say the least."

As they sat looking at each other, none of them knowing what to say next, Maggie's mobile phone chirped. She pulled it out of her tote and saw that it was from her co-worker. She said to the men, "I'm sorry, but I need to take this call."

She walked to the corner of the room where she said softly, but not softly enough to escape the priests' hearing. "Bruce, this isn't a good time. I'll call you back later."

"Maggie, get your sweet little ass over to Chelan," came the unwelcome voice through the receiver. "Your vacation is over. A lightning fire's started east of the mountains near Lake Chelan. It's time for you to go in."

"Is this an order from Mr. Stanley?"

"It's coming from me, sweet cheeks. Mr. Stanley is out of town so that makes me your immediate superior."

Bristling at his insolence, she said, "Oh no you're not my superior or my anything else. Don't ever make that mistake. I'm on vacation. Ask Patrick to go in and start questioning." The tone of her voice was full-on defiant.

"It's your job, Maggie, and we need you there, so get moving."

Maggie stood her ground. "I'll get there when I can but don't think for a minute it's because you told me to." Her tone remained firm.

"Well, you might not have a job when you return. Besides, baby cakes, I miss you." His voice dripped with insincere sweetness.

Maggie shuddered and spoke softly. "Bruce, don't ever try to threaten me. You have no control over my job and don't you forget it. I'll be in touch with Mr. Stanley for my assignments, not you." With that she clicked off and put the phone back in her tote. She was uncomfortably aware that the two priests were watching her and had heard her conversation.

"I am so embarrassed that you overheard this." She picked her cup up from a stack of books. Her hands were shaking.

"Father Francesco was the first to speak. "Who is this person, Maggie? Did he suggest he was going to fire you?"

"I work with him, but he's not my boss and he can't fire me."

Father Matthew, his body tense and his jaw locked in a grim line, took some long breaths and then spoke softly, "Don't listen to him, Maggie. No one has a right to bully you."

The tiniest smile escaped Father Francesco's lips. He turned to Maggie. "I hope you can stay, but we will understand if your job calls you away. If there is anything I can do, I will help you any way I can. Now, how about another cup of tea to settle our disquietude? Father Matthew, could you please refill the teapot?"

Father Matthew relaxed a little and returned to the kitchen, teapot in hand. While the water heated, he stole another quick look at the envelope. Why would it have been placed in such a curious spot?

CHAPTER EIGHTEEN

"You're sure the papers are well hidden, aren't you?" The bishop had insisted on meeting Father Francesco in the garden. The sun was setting and Bishop Davis liked to enjoy the garden in the evening when the winds abated. He sat on a bench, one arm draped over the back. The old priest stood before him.

"Yes, Excellency. They are well hidden." Father Francesco sighed as he reported to the bishop, evidence that he did not want to be there.

"Now what do we do about the young lady? How do we get her to stop this infernal snooping?" He grunted in obvious displeasure at the whole situation.

"She will go to Chelan soon. She has to collect data on the forest fire. Perhaps she won't come back."

The bishop gazed across the grounds and grumbled. "Short of death, you know very well she'll be back. She won't stop until she finds what she's looking for. I know her kind. They never quit."

"Eminence, I guess I don't understand why she can't know what happened." Father Francesco looked genuinely puzzled as he shifted back and forth seeking relief for his arthritic knees.

"Because, Father Francesco, it could harm the Church. And me." The bishop set his jaw.

"I don't understand how it could hurt you. It happened many years ago. No one remembers."

"I just don't like this woman digging around in our church business. Tell Father Matthew I want to see him." It was clear the bishop was terminating the conversation.

Father Francesco shuffled off in search of Father Matthew.

Bishop Davis strolled back to his office where he sat at his desk, deep in thought, blowing lazy circles with pipe smoke. As the sun had set, the room had a dusky hue about it. The bishop leaned back in his chair, folded his arms, and waited. He did not move when Father Matthew entered. "Father, do come in." His tone was surly.

"Eminence, you wanted to see me?" Father Matthew made no attempt to sit down but neither was he invited. Father Francesco had warned him that the bishop was in a churlish mood.

"I did. I have a new task for you. I understand the young lady is going to Chelan to study a fire. I want you to go there and keep an eye on her," he directed.

"What? Why?" Father Matthew did a double take in surprise.

"You are to convince her to drop the search for whatever happened to her aunt."

Matthew's surprise was evident when he said without hesitation, "Eminence, I don't understand. Is she some kind of threat to the Church?"

"Threat?" he sputtered. "Threat to the Church? Absolutely not. I just refuse to let her control this diocese and how we do business." The innocent question had pushed a volatile button with the cranky bishop.

Father Matthew started to challenge him, but then thought better of it. "What do you want me to do?" He didn't like whatever was happening.

"I already told you—you are to convince her that she must not come back and resume this blasted search of hers." The bishop's voice rose and his fist slammed the desk.

Father Matthew stammered, "I'm not sure this is feasible—I can't really follow her around in her line of work."

"Do whatever it takes. Just see that she doesn't come back. Now leave."

"What about my duties in Grand Coulee? I've already been away too long from my parish." Matthew's concern about his parishioners was just.

"I will send Father Stephen to take your calls and monitor any small problems that occur. He certainly knows how to say Mass. Anything else can wait." The bishop's tone was dismissive.

Father Matthew's face did not telegraph the outrage he felt. He thought of the visitations that needed to be made, the confessions that needed to be heard, the church business that needed attention in his parish. He would welcome Father Stephen's help for a few days, but this assignment was unreasonable.

"Eminence," he said with a hint of the requisite bow, and he took his leave.

CHAPTER NINETEEN

Father Matthew walked straight to Father Francesco's cottage. He stormed in the door without ceremony and sputtered, "I don't get it. What is he hiding? I can't leave my parish and stand around in a fire zone, just to keep a bishop happy." Father Matthew seethed, pacing in a small circle in Father Francesco's messy living room,

"Look at it this way Matthew, my lad, you would have the opportunity to see Maggie at a job she seems to enjoy. It seems not unlike what you did before you joined the priesthood. You chased after oil fires. She chases after tree and brush fires."

"True, but I have a parish in Grand Coulee I'm responsible for. It annoys me that I have to follow orders that are nonsensical and contrary to the essence of my vows to minister to those who need me. He asks me to abandon my parish to follow a woman into a fire in order to convince her to stay away from the very church she's come to for help."

"No, it doesn't seem logical," the old priest agreed. "But are you prepared to refuse a direct assignment from your bishop?"

"I'm afraid so, Father. I need to get back to my community—for my own spiritual health as well as theirs. I need to reconnect with my parish life. And I need to trust my bishop's motives."

Father Francesco looked upon his young friend's tortured face. He put his arm around the young man's shoulders. "My boy, your bishop, too, is troubled. I cannot explain it to you, but I think perhaps a toddy would be in order this evening."

"I think you're right, Father." The young priest's smile was weak. "May I do the honors?"

"I would be grateful. You know where to find everything." The old priest sank into his well-worn recliner and closed his eyes, as if he knew he would have time for a nice rest.

In the kitchen, Father Matthew opened the cupboard that held Father Francesco's bar glasses and his modest stash of alcohol. A manila envelope fell onto the counter; it had to have been positioned to fall when the cupboard door opened. Matthew was not surprised to see the date penned on the front—1936. This time he opened the envelope and pulled out the contents—a hand-written letter that began,

"To His Holiness, Pope Pius XI."
Via the Right Reverend Bishop Reynard Ryan
1936

I am writing this on behalf of several parishioners who are concerned about the behavior of Father_____. He has been observed having a soda with a young lady, walking with her around church grounds (on more than one occasion) and walking with her in Minnehaha Park. We understand that priests take a vow of chastity and are not to go off campus without another priest in attendance.

We demand that you look into the behavior of Father _____.

Prudence Pittock
And 16 faithful members.

The name of the offending priest had been cut from the letter, snipped out by scissors. By the time he had read the letter three times, Matthew's mind reeled with more questions, but one answer was becoming apparent. Maggie's quest was probably not a wild goose chase. He walked back into the living room and fanned the snoozing priest's face with the envelope. The old man opened his eyes with a start.

"Oh, my," he said. "I didn't hide that very carefully, did I? The bishop will be displeased." Father Francesco affected a chagrined expression.

"So Bishop Davis *is* purposely thwarting Maggie's search."

"Goodness, did I suggest that? Chalk it up to an old man's confusion," the old priest equivocated.

"Did this letter ever reach the pope, Father?"

"It would appear not, unless a carbon copy was sent by mistake."

"What does it mean?" asked Father Matthew.

Father Francesco gently retrieved the letter and said, "When Maggie comes back from Chelan, and she has reason to, we'll figure that out. Now go call her. We can wait for our toddy."

With that he struggled out of his chair and nudged Father Matthew out the door, making the sign of the cross at his retreating back.

CHAPTER TWENTY

Father Matthew called Maggie's mobile. "I need to get back to Grand Coulee in the morning. Could I hitch a ride when you decide to head to Chelan?"

"I would be happy to take you back to Grand Coulee. It seems there's no reason to stay here." Her voice carried the disappointment she felt that her search had dead-ended.

The priest rolled his eyes heavenward as he disobeyed the second directive the bishop had delivered. "I suggest you do the work you need to do in Chelan and then come back to Spokane." He would let her know about the letter when the time seemed right.

"We'll see. I'll pick you up in front of the cathedral. Will seven o'clock give you time for morning prayers?"

"Perfect," he answered.

"Are we going to stash you in the trunk so the bishop doesn't catch you riding with me?"

Father Matthew laughed. "Very funny, you trouble maker. I'll see you in the morning."

Morning dawned splendidly, bathing the city and the cathedral in fresh gold. Father Matthew, dressed in full priestly garb, tossed his bag into the back of Maggie's Civic and folded his long frame into the passenger seat. The conversation was limited until they were well out of Spokane on Highway 2. The side trip to Grand Coulee would add an hour and a half to the drive to Chelan but Maggie didn't mind at all.

Gazing across the landscape, she said, "There wasn't much here except rolling hills and sagebrush, before irrigation. Now look—wheat as far as you can see."

Matthew smiled. "It'll morph into sagebrush country up the road."

"But there's beauty in that, too," she said. "I like the way the light plays on the outcroppings and the hills. And I like to watch the dust devils skittering about."

He smiled at how comfortable he felt traveling with this woman who appreciated the stark landscape as much as he did. He said, "I thought parts of the Middle East were incredibly beautiful too, even though most people would say they're austere. What deserts have in common is lack of people. I think those who venture into the desert or high mountains do so in a search for the human spirit. For a while I thought that's what I loved about Iraq. Crawling up out of Africa into the birthplace of humanity, there were places where the terrain was so challenging it became spiritual."

Maggie nodded in agreement. "I understand what you're saying. The desert is mystical. I'd probably live in Arizona or New Mexico if I could stand the heat. I'm afraid I'm a sissy when the temperature climbs over a hundred ten on a daily basis."

"There was a lot of that in Iraq," he mused.

As they left the planted fields behind, they watched the desert roll by. An occasional pine dotted the landscape. "Look, Maggie, to the right. A pair of coyotes are watching us."

"They're watching for gumdrops."

"Gumdrops?"

"Mice," she laughed. "They're a coyote's major food source. These guys are the ultimate survivors, you know. They'll be here along with the cockroaches when the world ends, as long as the gumdrops hold up. Then they may take on a diet of cockroaches."

The miles ticked by while they simply enjoyed the beauty of the land and the comfortable silence until Father Matthew turned and said, "I have a couple of questions. Were you raised Catholic?"

"Yes and no. Dad didn't go to Mass, but he saw to it that we went to Catholic catechism. Mother was Protestant and she made us go to the Presbyterian Church."

"And your father didn't object?" Father Matthew looked puzzled.

"No. I guess he was pretty open-minded. I never told the priests, though—this was in the day when Catholics were not to set foot inside another church. My best friends were Catholic, so I leaned toward the Catholic Church, plus I loved the ritual of the Latin Mass."

Maggie rolled down her window and let the hot desert air fill the car. "Come on Matthew, let the wind blow your hair," she said and then blinked and startled when she realized she had called him by his name, alone.

Matthew rolled down his window and the awkward moment passed. Maggie picked up her story where she'd left off and Father Matthew leaned close to hear her over the wind noise.

"Dad was content to have us exposed to lots of ideas and let us do our own thinking and deciding about religion. He became a Mason and Mom was in Eastern Star. In fact, he led DeMolay for many years."

"That's not very Catholic," Father Matthew observed and Maggie agreed.

"To be honest, I couldn't tolerate the hypocrisy of the Presbyterians. Sunday was show and tell day for new clothes, fine furs, and jewelry. The minister preached 'honor thy spouse,' and everyone knew he was having a fling with his secretary. I tried a lot of different churches, but none stuck." She paused and looked across the car at him. "Enough of that. What is the other question?"

Looking out the window, Father Matthew asked, "Do you still go to Mass?"

"I do. Not regularly."

"Why do you think that is?"

"That's an extra question, Father," Maggie teased. "I think my Dad's relationship with the Church rubbed off on me. He loved it because it's what he knew, but hated it, I think, because whatever transpired in the family affected how he viewed religion. Ironically, he always wanted to send us to Catholic schools because the Jesuits offered the best education. We never did go as kids, but when it counted, I chose Seattle U, all the way through my Doctorate. Dad won that one!" Maggie smiled at him.

"So you're really a sometime Catholic."

"You caught me, Father." She grinned. "But I've never missed a Christmas midnight Mass. Imagine that!"

"I'd like to imagine you at Mass every Sunday."

It was spoken with gentle humor, but he saw Maggie draw in her breath and square her shoulders.

"Maybe, if I thought the Catholic Church really cared about me. Look at your bishop. Do I matter to him? No. He isn't even civil toward me."

The priest couldn't defend Bishop Davis, but he was compelled to defend the Church. "Bishop Davis doesn't represent the whole Church, Maggie."

"No, but he represents the parts I've seen."

The priest recoiled and fell silent, as if she had slapped him. In essence, she had. He could have told her about the letter in the manila envelope, but he didn't.

She made the turn into Grand Coulee and drove straight to St. Francis Church.

The Civic rolled around the statuary garden and stopped in front of the church. Father Matthew got out of the car and took his bag from the back seat. He walked around to the driver's side and said, "Have faith in Father Francesco, Maggie. I know he's trying to help."

"I don't have much faith in anyone anymore," she snapped, her tone edged with cynicism.

"Well, stay safe and let me know when you can get back to our pursuit of the mysterious Great-aunt Milly." He stepped back from the car.

She nodded and barely waited until he picked up his bag before she pulled out into the street, leaving him to stare after her.

Maggie glanced at the priest in her rear view mirror and chastised herself for being so abrupt with him. What's the matter with me? She thought. He had been nothing but helpful. "*Our* pursuit," he'd just said. And I enjoy his company. Too much? She put that thought out of her mind as quickly as it had come in. She was on her way to work.

CHAPTER TWENTY-ONE

As soon as she was out of sight of the church, Maggie pulled over to turn on her phone and check in with her boss. When Mr. Stanley heard her voice he said, urgency in his voice, "Please, Maggie, get there as fast as you can. Find out what you can at the base camp then go in as far as it's safe. You know the drill. Check on the equipment that's already there—planes, trucks, and how much more they expect to bring in. Are they using a retardant? Where did the fire start? How did it start? Do they have fire jumpers on duty? Just be careful, Maggie. I don't want anything to happen to you."

"Got it, Boss. I'll keep in touch. I think the slant will be on surviving fires and what people need to do to prepare for them. I'm on my way."

"Good. Oh, call your brother. He's called twice, trying to track you down. You haven't been answering."

Maggie called Lucas. He picked up on the first ring. "Hey, Brother" she said, "I'm heading for Chelan. Should be getting to base camp in two or three hours."

Lucas said, "It's about time you called." She could hear the relief in his voice.

"Not to worry, Lucas, but I might not have good coverage over there, so stay in touch with Mr. Stanley. He'll know what's going on." She hesitated and then went on. "Lucas, if anything happens to me, please call Father Matthew at St. Francis Church in Grand Coulee."

"Father? Why should I let a priest know what you're doing?"

"Because he is supposed to be keeping track of me for the bishop and Lord knows, I don't want to upset a bishop."

"Is this the same bishop that won't tell you anything?"

"It is, but don't take it out on Father Matthew. He's a good guy. He's helping me sort out Milly's story, which, by the way, is beginning to look like it never happened."

"Very interesting. I'd say I told you so, but you'd say obscene things to me. Okay, so I'm supposed to call this priest to let him know if you croak." She knew he was grinning, but her silence told him she was not.

Lucas snickered, as he always did when he got under her skin. "I think I'll call now so he has plenty of time to worry about you in the fire."

"No, Lucas. Only call if something bad happens."

"Okay, Sis. I'm going to drive over now. Take good care of yourself, Maggie. Be sure you have a fireproof tent. I love you and don't want to lose my favorite sister."

"I love you, too, Lucas, but you don't have to come over now. I'm just going to base camp. There's nothing dangerous in that. Please tell Mom as little as possible so she doesn't worry."

"What am I supposed to tell him, the priest? You're dead, you're in love with him, you like coffee rather than tea? What?"

"Lucas!" Maggie half laughed, half sputtered.

"No worries, Sis. I'll take care of things. You take care of yourself."

Maggie heard the phone click and thought how lucky she was to have Lucas for her brother. He knew her so well, maybe even better than she knew herself.

CHAPTER TWENTY-TWO

It was close to noon when Maggie arrived at the base camp. Smoke hung in a haze, enough to cause her eyes to itch. She walked up to the man who appeared to be in charge. He was at least six foot seven, and she guessed he had a military crew cut under his cap. He was waving directions to a crew of smoke jumpers heading out for their plane. She marveled that these men and women would jump out of a plane into a fire, and she wondered how they could stand the smoke when they were in the midst of it.

She held out her hand. "Hi, I'm Maggie Callahan. I'm the reporter here to gather data about the fire." The man's hand was huge, his grasp firm. She thought she might not survive the handshake.

"I'm Ted," he bellowed, a scowl on his face. "Where's your boss? Why isn't he here?" Maggie could see he was not pleased. "I don't usually help the press. I'm surprised he sent a woman."

Maggie took a step back. Her sigh was audible. "I am also the statistician. I collect the data for agencies including the Forest Service. I'm the one you want on the job now so you're better equipped for the next fire. You have female fire fighters on the lines. Just think of me as a slightly different kind of fire fighter." She could see he wasn't convinced. "I'm trained to do this."

"Yeah, well the game has changed a little. It looks like we have a lost child somewhere around the Ten Mile Creek campground and I won't be able to pull together a search and rescue team for hours."

"A lost child? This is your lucky day. I'm trained for search and rescue. EMT, too." She could see him relax a bit, his reservations beginning to break down.

"If that's so, I may have to send you in to get a head start looking for the kid."

"It's so, and I'm ready to go. But first I need to get some information from you," she said.

Ted leaned against the side panel of a pickup and faced her, answering each question. He ended by telling her what he knew about the lost child, which wasn't much. "The parents called the sheriff a couple of hours ago, but we haven't heard any more and we can't get a call through to them. All we know is the kid disappeared while they were packing up to leave the camp."

Maggie was satisfied he accepted her and her role here. "Now I need to go on in," she said.

"I'll give you this truck," he said, pointing to the blue pickup beside them. "You know how to drive a 4 by 4?"

"I do."

"There's a fire jacket in the cab. It's big enough for two of you, but it'll do. You have boots in there, too. You have a walkie-talkie or mobile phone? That may be the most important piece of equipment you have."

"I have a mobile phone. It's charged but you never know if it has reception in this kind of terrain."

"I'll give you a good map and a walkie-talkie, but sometimes they don't work in the mountains, either. Now, let's check out your gear." He turned to a young man waiting for orders. "Larry, would you get the young lady a tent and outfit a pack for her?" He turned to Maggie and said, "You'll have all the equipment you need—knife, gloves, goggles, foam, flashlight, binoculars. The truck has a pump and hose, and is full of water, although I hope you won't need them. Go on over to the food truck and pick enough to feed yourself for forty-eight hours. You never know what will happen."

"Thanks, Ted. I'll get everything back safe and sound." The two of them had come to an understanding. The hostility was gone in the face of potential danger.

The food truck looked like a mobile barbecue pit and smelled so good she realized she was hungry. She selected sandwiches of barbecued pork, chicken and beef. The fruit all looked fresh, so she took apples, bananas and oranges. And many bottles of water. Ted followed her over.

"Your diet looks good for somebody sitting at a desk. Take lots of brownies and hunks of pie. You are going to need major carbohydrates before you're done." He loaded the sweets into her pack.

"You sound like you think I'm going to be out there for several days," Maggie said as she moved toward the truck.

"You never know. We always go prepared. We sure as hell don't want to lose a novice in the middle of a search and rescue." His eyes told her he was genuinely concerned. Maggie smiled.

"I'm not a novice," she said and Ted bobbed his head up and down in acknowledgment.

"Remember, the road runs out of pavement in about six miles. The dirt road leads to where the hiking trails begin and will end up at the campground on Ten Mile Creek, where the kid's family is looking for him, last I heard. A few people live deep in the forest. Hopefully everyone is out, but if you do see anyone, tell them to get out. And be extra careful on the dirt road. It's rutty and you have to slow down. Beware of trees and brush close to the road. There's a lot of pine and bone dry vegetation in there. If it catches fire close to you, turn around and head back. This is a hot spot. It'll burn fast. Why don't you call me every half hour so I know you're all right? If you can't do that, I will assume you are caught in the fire." With his hand on the rolled down window and an earnest look in his eyes, Maggie was sure he must be a father thinking about sending his own daughter on a dangerous mission. "Maggie, above all, keep yourself safe."

"I will, thanks." Tennyson's poem came to mind: *Into the valley of death rode the six hundred.* Hope that's not me, the Light Brigade. Very light, she thought grimly.

CHAPTER TWENTY-THREE

As she drove away from safety and food, she thought about Father Matthew. She asked herself why she had been rude to him. She knew her sarcasm had been biting. She knew she liked his company and found it difficult to separate her feelings from the fact that he was a priest and unavailable. These were perilous thoughts. She must think of something else.

Maggie stopped at every house along the country road, noting whether anyone was home and whether animals were in view. At one home she found three horses in the field. She tried the mobile phone. It worked.

"There's a place here with nobody home and three horses in the field. Can someone come out and get them?"

"I'll call the sheriff." Ted responded.

Once Maggie hit the dirt road, she slowed to a crawl and passed homes that had been evacuated. She was pleased to note that most people had removed combustible materials from around their home sites. The tree line around most homes was well back from the structures. Some had metal roofs. Good. In one yard she saw a coiled hose near a goat barn. Somebody had the right idea, but she knew that small hose wouldn't stop a forest fire. She noticed that the farther into the woods she drove, most houses still had some type of composition roofs rather than metal. Some even had cedar shakes. She shook her head and made a note in the notebook beside her: Mandatory—metal roofs.

She turned a corner into a large open meadow. It had burned three years before. Charred trees stood at attention and most of the vegetation was low to the ground. Looking across the meadow to what must be the creek bed, Maggie could see flames along the canyon walls on the far side. She called Ted.

"Your duty now is to search for the lost kid," he said, "We can worry about home owners later. When the four o'clock winds begin to blow, the fire will move fast."

"Ted, I haven't seen any wildlife. Not even birds."

"Animals don't usually move until the heat drives them out. If you see animals on the move, you're in trouble." As if she didn't know, Maggie thought.

"How far in is the campground?" she asked.

"It should be about five more miles. The creek is wide and fast there."

As they talked, Maggie could see a plane dropping retardant over the far canyon. "I see one plane working the fire across the canyon right now, Ted. Are they likely to send in a helicopter for a child?"

"Only if he's injured and needs immediate attention. Not at night, though."

Maggie caught the implication—time was precious. "Thanks. I'll check in again when I get to the campground. Hopefully I can still get you." She hung up and gunned the truck toward the campground. Twenty minutes later the last thing she expected to see were two people standing beside a car. They waved frantically for her to stop.

They were young, probably late teens, and dressed for a day at the beach, in sandals and shorts.

Maggie stopped. "What happened?"

The young man started to explain, and Maggie could hear panic in his voice. "We were camping at Ten Mile Creek. When we woke up and smelled the smoke, we decided to get out of there."

"But then this couple couldn't find their little boy and they asked us to help look for him," the girl broke in. "We've been looking all morning."

The boy took over. "Penny and Evan—that's the couple—made a call from their mobile phone, but the phone went out right after that. So they asked us if we could drive out and send back help for them. You know, like search and rescue people."

"But then we hit a huge pothole too fast and the car just died on us." Tears were in the young woman's voice.

Maggie interrupted the tag team narrative, hoping to calm the young people. "I'm Maggie Callahan," she said. "And you are?"

"Jason Sweet," said the boy. "Susan Pfeiffer," said the girl, adding, "My parents don't know we're together and my father is going to kill me." She burst into tears.

"Okay, Susan, we'll worry about that later," Maggie smiled. "For now let's worry about that little boy and getting everyone out of here safely." The young people nodded and Jason put his arm around Susan.

"The good news is, you found me! I'm trained in search and rescue." Maggie tried to achieve a light note, but the gravity of the situation made it difficult. "How far are we from that campground?"

"Maybe a mile," Jason answered. "But the road is awful. You can't go fast."

"I understand," Maggie said. "Here's what we're going to do. I'll give you some food, and you wait right here by your car. I'm going to send that family out and they'll stop to pick you up. Hopefully they'll have their little boy with them. Get everything of value out of your car. The next time you see it, there may be nothing left but a shell."

Maggie looked across the meadow. The fire burned in the tops of the trees along the canyon walls, but it was still on the other side. She gave food and water to the young people.

"How much do you know about forest fires?" Susan asked.

"Enough to know we want to be out of here before the four o'clock winds pick up. Once it gets into the meadow it'll move very fast and engulf everything in its way."

"Will Evan and Penny be here by then?" Jason's eyes were enormous with fear.

"Count on it," replied Maggie, hoping she was right as she climbed into the truck and started the engine. "Have a good lunch," she shouted and waved.

Bumping along at a snail's pace was taking a toll on Maggie's nerves, and she had to look closely for the entrance to the campground. The smoke was thickening. At last she spotted it and a lone SUV parked beside one of the campsites. "Contact!" she thought and noted it was two-thirty. She picked up the phone to check in with Ted and her breath caught: "No Service" flashed in red. She'd known this was likely to happen, but she hadn't predicted her feeling of total abandonment. No time to dwell on it. She would try the walkie-talkie later, but she didn't hold out much hope for it, either. She climbed out of the truck and lifted her pack out of the bed. She heaved it onto her back, adjusted the straps, and started walking.

"Okay, God, if you're there—"she said aloud, and as she said it a man, a woman and a young girl climbed up the bank from the creek. She blinked, as if by doing so she would see a little boy with them. It didn't work and a thought slipped through her mind that God might not be on the job today.

The woman broke into a run and the man was a few paces behind, carrying his daughter. The woman reached Maggie first.

"Oh thank God you're here!" Her head turned from one side to the other, her eyes scanning the distance behind Maggie. "Where is the rest of the team?" she asked, her voice carrying the desperation she felt.

"Penny?" Maggie asked as she dropped her pack.

"Yes, yes. Penny Pointer. But where are the others?" the woman demanded. Her husband stood by her side, their daughter in his arms.

"Okay, I'm glad you're here, safe." Maggie kept her voice low and calm. "You need to know I'm trained in search and rescue, and I'm going to find your little boy."

Evan took up the question. "But aren't there more people coming?"

"I'm it," Maggie admitted. Penny began to cry. Maggie knew she had to take charge. Immediately.

"Maggie Callahan," she said to Evan, over Penny's loud sobs. He shifted the weight of the child and Maggie grasped his outstretched hand firmly. "And you're Evan?" He nodded.

The little girl put out her hand, "I'm Ruthie," she announced, and Maggie smiled.

Maggie addressed Penny. "Mrs. Pointer, we must all stay in control now. I need to know more about your son. His name?"

Penny heaved a shuddering breath and answered, "Jon. He's only six. I was—we were—packing up when he disappeared. I swear, I only took my eyes off him a minute. "Penny broke into sobs again. Evan put Ruthie down and comforted his wife. Ruthie wrapped herself around his leg for security. Maggie understood their emotions.

When Maggie had learned what Jon was wearing, what color his hair was, what had interested him most about the camp area, and his nickname, Jon-O, she was ready to explain her plan.

"Mr. and Mrs. Pointer, I am going to search for Jon. You are going to take Ruthie and drive out of here. Go back to the base camp just outside of Chelan."

Penny's reaction was predictable. "Are you out of your mind?" she screamed. "We can't leave Jon. He's our child for God's sake." Maggie looked at the little girl hugging her father's leg, thankful that she had not followed her brother. "I'm not leaving here without Jon. He's my baby." Penny's voice rose in a wail and her knees gave out.

Evan knelt beside her in the long grass, rubbing her back with one hand, the other arm wrapped around Ruthie. He looked up a Maggie. "I, uh, I don't think we can—"

"You don't have a choice, Mr. Pointer," she said, her voice hard. "I am trained for this. You are not. I can take care of myself and Jon when I find him, but I don't have the time or the equipment to take care of you as well. You would be a hindrance that could jeopardize us all."

She could see that Evan knew she was right. He spoke a few words quietly to his wife and then helped her rise from the ground. Maggie didn't want to take time to return to the campground, so she made sure they had food and water in their vehicle and told them about Jason and Susan waiting for them along the road.

"Don't waste any time," she instructed. "It's nearly three o'clock and you want to be a long way from here by four. When you get to the base camp, report to Ted. You can tell him I'm fine and I'll keep trying to call in—I may find pockets where I can get reception."

Penny just nodded and clasped Maggie's hand. "God be with you," she choked out before she started to sob again. Evan lifted Maggie's pack and remarked how heavy it was as he helped her slide into the straps.

"It has everything I need to keep Jon and me safe," she said. "Including brownies and apple pie." They exchanged a wisp of a smile before he turned to gather up his wife and daughter.

"I don't know what to say, Miss Callahan—"

"Don't worry. I'll bring Jon back to you."

"Yes, I believe you will," he said.

Maggie watched them walk away from her. She raised her hand in a farewell wave they did not see, and then she spoke again to God. "Please let me keep my promise," she whispered.

CHAPTER TWENTY-FOUR

Maggie walked along the bank, stumbling over rocks and grass for about a half mile when she saw them. He was on an island in the middle of the creek, happily throwing rocks. Dressed in shorts, a tee-shirt and sandals, he was oblivious to the smoke and the patches of fire burning across the creek. Standing beside him was a brown mare, her nose down next to his head.

Maggie stopped and stared. If it hadn't been for the smoke haze surrounding them, it would have been a perfect camera shot. "Hi Jon," Maggie shouted. "I'm Maggie. Looks like you're having fun."

The boy looked up and waved.

"How did you get out into the middle of the creek?" she called

Jon smiled. "I walked on rocks," he said, and pointed downstream. Maggie could see where rocks had formed a tiny peninsula into the creek. "Narnia walked across from the other side."

She threw her backpack on the ground and picked her way across the slippery rocks. "Hey, Jon-O, I've come to take you to your mom and dad."

"We can't leave Narnia behind," Jon said emphatically.

"Is that the name of your friend?" Maggie looked at the mare. She was shaggy even for a hot summer day, a sign that she had not been cared for in a long time. Yet she appeared to be calm.

"I named her for the books my dad reads to me." He reached up and patted the horse's nose.

"The Chronicles of Narnia were my favorite stories when I was young, too." Maggie reached out and stroked the mare's nose. The horse nickered, but made no attempt to run. Had the fire gentled her? Too bad I don't know the horse, she thought. Jon could ride her out. Wishful thinking on my part. You can't put a child you don't know on a horse you don't know.

"Where are my mom and dad?" Jon seemed to suddenly realize where he was and he looked like he was going to cry.

"Your mom and dad are back there, waiting. They asked me to look for you."

"Are you a forest ranger?" Jon asked "I always wanted to meet Smokey the Bear. I don't like all the smoke, though. It hurts my eyes."

"Tell you what," Maggie said, as she reached for his hand and started back for the shore, "you and I and Narnia are going to walk out of here and go to your mom and dad." Maggie walked away holding the boy's hand. The mare followed.

Once on the bank, Maggie took another look at the trees. The fire was still in the tops of the distant trees, but she knew that would change as soon as the wind came up. She heaved the pack onto her back. "You and I are going to do something fun. It's the old run/walk game. We are going to run and walk and I'm going to hold your hand the entire way. Can you do that?"

"Sure, Maggie." He grabbed her hand as if he would never let go.

"Let's go, Bucko." They made surprisingly good time, and the horse followed along. At the old picnic table, Maggie set down the backpack and checked the mare. The horse waited quietly to find out what would come next.

"I'm hungry," Jon announced. "And my eyes hurt. Narnia doesn't like the smoke either."

"I know. We're going to get out of here, but first—" She pulled two sandwiches out of the backpack. "How about a roast beef sandwich? And I have lots of apples. Let's give one to Narnia."

"Yes, Narnia should have some apple, but I don't like roast beef." Jon wrinkled his nose.

Maggie smiled. "Well, young man, it's that or starve."

"I guess today I like roast beef sandwiches." Maggie gave an apple to Narnia who stood quietly and chewed.

What am I going to do with this mare? Maggie wondered as she hustled the boy into the truck, eager to get moving. I could tie her to the truck, but I'd have to drive three miles an hour all the way out. Can't do that. Too slow. Gotta get out of here fast. She buckled Jon's seatbelt.

"What about Narnia?" Jon asked, concern showing on his little smoke stained face.

"She'll follow us," Maggie said with more confidence than she felt. "We'll drive slowly so she can keep up." This trip is going to be touch and go, Maggie thought.

They drove in silence while Maggie slowly increased the speed and the horse trotted along behind, unimpeded by the potholes. Jon spent most of the time peering around the side of his seat to catch glimpses of Narnia. It was after four o'clock when she spotted the young couples' old car through the thickening smoke haze at the side of the road. It would be four hours before the sun would set, but it already seemed like twilight. She tried to relax a little, so she began to make small talk with Jon. He was the first to see deer coming out of the smoke bank ahead. "Look! Five deers," he shouted. "No, six, no seven deers!"

Maggie stopped the truck. In an instant the deer bounded by them, not reacting at all to the truck facing them or the horse who had begun to neigh. Then she saw a badger, and in a mini-second her eyes focused on a wave of small creatures running away from the fire that must have jumped the creek.

Jon clapped his hands and bounced up and down on the seat, delighted with the parade of animals. Maggie grabbed her phone and prayed the "No Service" light wasn't blinking. It wasn't.

"Thank God, Maggie—I've called every five minutes and couldn't get through," shouted Ted when he heard her voice.

"Let's not waste any time. I have Jon," she said, neglecting to mention the horse, "and we seem to be heading into the fire. Please tell me there's another way out of here."

"There is—it'll take you in the opposite direction of the base camp, all the way to Alta Lake."

"I'm for it." She picked up her notebook and pencil. "Fire away!" she said. The irony escaped her and she wondered why Ted snickered.

When she was sure she understood the complicated route through the park and over the creek that would lead her to the road on the other side, Maggie began to turn the truck around and Jon cried out, "Narnia! Don't run over Narnia!"

"She's smart, Jon—she'll get out of the way." Jon began to cry, but Maggie had to concentrate on maneuvering the truck without getting stuck in the roadside brush. Finally headed in the right direction, she got out to check the mare who had already turned around and seemed anxious to follow the wildlife back to the creek.

"Sorry, girl—we'll have to backtrack, but I expect you already know that." Narnia lifted her head, neighed and then snorted several times. She looked like she would be willing to lead this time, but allowed Maggie to walk her to the back of the truck. Maggie couldn't imagine why she had not bolted with the rest of the animals, and she sent a little prayer that she and Jon would not have to bolt and leave Narnia behind.

Maggie climbed back into the drivers' seat. "Here we go, Jon-O."

Jon's eyelids began to droop and flicker, but he kept up his vigilant watch for Narnia, smartly picking her way along behind them.

CHAPTER TWENTY-FIVE

Lucas stood next to his beat up old Ford pickup. He'd driven the old girl across the Cascades a little harder than he should have, and she needed water. Grabbing an empty milk jug out of the truck bed, he looked around for a faucet. He was filling the jug when a loud voice asked, "Are you Lucas?"

Lucas spun around. "I am. How'd you know?"

"Your hair. You have curly red hair just like Maggie. I'm Ted."

Lucas hastily cleaned his hand on his pant leg before he extended it for the obligatory handshake.

"First, I hope you know I tried to talk her out of going into the fire area," Ted said.

Lucas smiled. "I know. When Maggie's on the job she does what needs to be done, and she doesn't take orders very well. She'll be fine."

"I might agree," said Ted, "except she went through a grassy, tree lined area that caught before she could turn around and get back." Lucas watched the men standing by their trucks and noted their equipment—pickaxes, fireproof coats, water barrels and hoses. These were firefighters, not search and rescue. Suddenly he was alert to what Ted was saying. Maggie could be in danger.

"Have you heard from her? Do you know where she is?" Lucas felt his throat constrict and his heartbeat begin to pound in his ears.

"Just talked to her and she's turning around. She has the boy with her." Seeing Lucas's puzzled frown, Ted explained about Maggie's rescue of the lost child.

Lucas swallowed hard and said, "Is there anything I can do to help? Just point me to what you need done." Lucas looked at all the crew Ted was overseeing and had an overpowering feeling he should call Father Matthew.

"I'll catch up with you," he said to Ted. "Do you have a phone I can use?" Ted handed him his mobile phone with a warning to get it right back to him. Lucas unfolded a piece of paper with the priest's number on it and dialed.

"Father Matthew?" Lucas said, anxiety in his voice.

"Yes. May I help you?" The voice sounded warm and welcoming.

"I'm Lucas Callahan, Father. Maggie asked me to call you if things got iffy over here at Chelan. She's gone into the fire zone to rescue a lost child and it looks like she's going to have trouble getting out. She's well trained in survival stuff, but I'm nervous and I thought she'd want me to let you know."

"Where are you?" Matthew asked, his voice a totally different tone. It signaled genuine concern and apprehension.

"I'm at the base camp just west of Chelan. That's the jump-off spot for fire fighters. Knowing my sister, she's all right, and I'm probably panicking, but I wanted you to be aware."

"I'll be there as soon as I can find a ride."

"Don't you have a car?"

"I do, but I have to leave it for the priest who will sit in for me while I'm gone." He lied for a reason he could not have easily justified, even to himself. "Don't worry, I'll be there."

Father Matthew returned the phone to its base, put his elbows on the desk, and cradled his head between his hands. He was having feelings he should not have. He recovered his composure and picked up the phone to call Glen Blackburn whose hunting cabin was near Chelan.

"Sure, I can go right away, Father. I need to make sure the cabin's not in danger, anyway. Maybe wet things down good."

"Thanks, Glen. I'll be waiting." Matthew hurried to his quarters to change into jeans and hiking boots. He put toiletries and a change of clothes into a backpack, threw a vest on over his black clerical shirt, and picked up his sacraments kit. His years of courting danger in the desert had taught him it was best to be prepared for anything.

Glen's foot rested heavy on the accelerator and two hours later they drove into the base camp. Matthew slung his backpack over his shoulder, picked up the sacraments case, and strode into the sea of people milling about the area. A woman pointed out Ted who was directing everybody's traffic.

"I'm Father Matthew Brannigan, a friend of Maggie Callahan," he said. "I'm here to help however I can." He stood almost eye to eye with Ted, lacking perhaps an inch.

Astonished, Ted blinked at the priest. In all the years he'd worked on the fire lines, a priest had never asked to help. He wasn't about to look a gift horse in the mouth.

"You bet, Father Brannigan. The cook needs help. We're feeding a pot load of firefighters here plus a lot of folks who've come out of the fire zone. Tell Jimmy I sent you over." Ted turned back to the smoke jumpers.

"Wait!" Matthew said.

Ted preempted his question. "Find Lucas," he called over his shoulder. "He'll fill you in on Maggie."

Father Matthew walked toward the food truck. A young man, his back to him, was lugging water jugs to the food truck. The hair was curly and red.

Lucas was lost in thought when he turned around and saw the man moving toward him. "I'll bet you are Father Matthew," he said, putting down the jugs and stretching his back as he put out his hand in greeting. "The white collar's a dead giveaway."

"I am and you are Lucas. The red hair's a dead giveaway." They both laughed. "Thanks again for the call. What's the latest news on Maggie?"

Lucas turned serious and reported Maggie's situation. "No communication since she turned around at four-thirty. Teams were sent in to fight the meadow fire, but the wind was up and the fire was spreading east and north, the direction Maggie was going. If she could get on the other side of the creek where it narrowed down north of the campground, she'd be in pretty good shape. But nightfall was approaching and it would be easy to get lost on the roads, which were little more than trails past the camp ground." Matthew listened, his jaw muscles tense.

"Father, I am glad you're here," Lucas said in a rush of gratitude he wasn't sure he understood. "Let's get working. It's easier for me to not think about Maggie if I have something to do."

Me too, thought Matthew.

CHAPTER TWENTY-SIX

Maggie drove as fast as she dared over the dry road. The ruts, angling one way and then the other, were all that identified it as a road. Ted had told her to wind along the north side of the camp ground toward the creek, take a left on the track that ran alongside the creek, and go about seven miles to the shallows where she could drive across. Narnia was keeping up with their slow pace, but Maggie knew she had to find a safe spot to stop so the horse could drink and rest.

——She'd made the left onto another rutted track. After she'd left the campground, the pine trees became more dense. Fodder for fire, she thought and then her thoughts wandered to Father Matthew. She found comfort in thinking about him. Comfort and something else she had no right to feel. In an effort to squelch those pesky feelings, she tried to call Ted every few minutes, but she had no mobile service and the walkie-talkie had been out of range back at the campground.

At six and a half miles after her turn onto the creek side trail, Maggie began to strain her eyes for signs of the shallow creek crossing. Between the onset of dusk and the smoke haze, it was impossible to distinguish between shallow water and deep water. She could hardly risk driving the truck into unknown depths, and she had no desire to walk in to test the depth and risk leaving Jon on his own. At eight miles, the creek had widened and the rutted trail had all but vanished, so she was sure she had passed the ford. She stopped to let Narnia munch grass and drink from the slow-moving creek. She reviewed her options while Jon was happily occupied with the horse.

It was nearly dark. She could backtrack and hope to find the crossing in the dark, or they could bed down here, an extra mile further away from the fire and hope—no, pray the fire wouldn't catch up with them. She knew the fire fighters would have been on the job until darkness set in, and she could only hope they had controlled the blaze or at least slowed it down. She hadn't seen planes in the air for hours, perhaps because of the strong winds which would be hazardous for smoke jumpers and would scatter fire retardant and make it useless. The breeze was gentle now, a good sign, but smoke was still thick, either because the wind had been pushing it in from the southwest for hours or because the fire was close. She didn't see embers flickering against the darkened sky. This should be a good sign, but it might be because the smoke obscured them. What to do?

Narnia approached, apparently sated, with Jon at her side, sagging more with every step. "I'm hungry," he whimpered and dropped to the grass beside her. The little fellow was exhausted and seemed near tears. She made her decision.

"Tell you what, Jon," she said. "Let's have a campout here. We'll eat in the dark, and I have a funny little silver tent we can use if we decide we need it."

"Can we build a fire?" he asked, and Maggie laughed when he answered his own question. "Oh, I guess that'd be a dumb idea."

"We don't need a fire. We have sandwiches and apples—"

"For Narnia?" he interrupted.

"Yes, for us, too. But here's the best part—we have brownies and apple pie."

He sat up. "Brownies? Do I have to eat a roast beef sandwich?"

"Naw," Maggie answered. "But you're going to have to eat extra apple pie." She could see his beaming smile through the darkness.

By flashlight, Maggie spread their evening meal out on the flame-retardant tarp that was part of her firefighter's pack. When they had eaten their fill and treated the horse to an apple, she pulled the piece of equipment out that no firefighter wants to use—the reflective aluminum shelter, the "fireproof tent" Lucas had spoken of earlier, back when it seemed like a joke. It was about the size of a coffin, she noted, but big enough for the two of them if they had to use it.

"Okay, Jon-O, we're going to have a little game of Get in the Lunchbox." She rolled the shelter out and they both jumped in, counting to see how long it took to zip it up and close themselves inside. Jon stopped counting at 21 because he was giggling so hard. They went through the drill two more times until Maggie was satisfied they would know what to do if it became necessary.

The tarp served as their bed. She placed the shelter beside her along with the spray cans of foam and the flashlight. She rolled up the big firefighter's gloves, one inside the other, as a pillow for Jon. The great firefighter's jacket would serve as a blanket for both of them when the night chill set in. She lay next to him, their sides touching. She imagined the smoke was subsiding a bit, but knew it was probably just because the air next to the ground was easier to breathe. She felt his little body relax and then snap back to attention as he struggled to stay awake.

"Will Narnia run away if I go to sleep?" he finally asked, revealing the reason he fought the sleep he desperately needed. It had been a long, hard day for a little boy.

"Not to worry. She'll be with us when you wake up."

Jon turned to snuggle closer to Maggie. In seconds he was asleep, but moments later he sat upright and in a tiny voice he asked, "Maggie, do you think we will burn up in the fire?"

Maggie put her arm around the little boy and said. "No, Jon. We'll wake up in the morning and go see your mommy and daddy." Sleep soon captured him. I hope I'm right, she thought. And she settled into a sleepless night watching for embers and listening for the roar of a forest burning nearby.

CHAPTER TWENTY-SEVEN

After an afternoon of hauling water and enormous bags of supplies and then making sandwiches as fast as the firefighters and evacuees could eat them, Lucas and Father Matthew ended the day making chocolate brownies in a huge kettle vat. The field kitchen was well stocked and equipped but there had been little time for talking or eating. When darkness closed in around the base camp and Jimmy told them they were finished for the day, each collapsed at a folding table with a plateful of the food they'd been preparing and a cup of coffee.

The day's labors had kept time moving fast, but every hour that had passed without word from Maggie had multiplied their thoughts about her and where she might be. Between bites, Matthew asked Lucas, "How long has Maggie chased after disasters?" It helped to say her name and open a conversation about her.

"As long as I can remember," Lucas chuckled. "She was always bringing home stray animals that were broken and needed tending. She would go to the library and check out books to find out how to fix them. Things she couldn't fix became a problem because our parents didn't want to take all those strays to a vet. Finally they put a stop to it, so she made friends with the vet and volunteered to help out at his clinic." He grinned wistfully, thinking about his soft-hearted sister.

Ted ambled over, looking like he hadn't slept in days, which was probably pretty accurate. "Okay, you two, things'll be quieting down here—not much we can do at night, and everyone needs some sleep."

Matthew and Lucas looked at each other as if neither wanted to ask the question. Finally Matthew broke the uncomfortable silence. "Where do you think Maggie is?" he asked.

"Well, we've had no contact with her since she had to turn around and run from the fire, but that's not necessarily bad news. It tells me she's probably crossed the creek and taken the road over to the lake I told her about and probably there's no mobile phone coverage there. More than likely, she decided to camp out at Alta Lake, rather than try to find her way back here in the dark. It's pretty remote up there. If we don't hear from her we'll go looking for her in the morning. She seems like a resourceful gal, and she's got that little boy to take care of. She's not going to let him down." He said it with a smile that belied his anxiety.

They both laughed softly—just enough to be polite. "That's Maggie," Lucas smiled, but his smile did not conceal his concern.

"Nothing we can do now," Ted said. "Try to catch some sleep. If the wind stays down we may see some let-up tomorrow. You might put in a plug with You-Know-Who for rain, Father." Ted raised his arm and pointed upward.

"I'll do that." Father Matthew promised Ted's retreating back. He turned to Lucas. "I guess we need a place to lie down," he said, looking around for a likely spot.

"How about my truck. Not very comfortable, but it's close to the action in case they hear something from Maggie."

"Great." Father Matthew followed him to the battered truck. "I've slept in worse."

"I have a couple of old beach blankets in the back. They're kind of nasty, but good enough keep the cold out. I'll take the cab and you can stretch out in the back. There's a canvas pup tent you can unfold, to lie on."

"Ah, five-star accommodations," Matthew grinned.

Lucas pulled the tent and the beach blankets from the back of the truck and they consigned themselves to their makeshift beds, aware that their concern for Maggie would interfere with sleep far more than the dismal sleeping arrangements.

Father Matthew pulled his rosary out of his pocket.

As the night wore on, minute by long minute, Maggie told herself stories to fight the need for sleep. She heard Narnia snuffle and then lie down, probably to catch the cleaner air at ground level. Smart horse. She laughed silently so as not to waken Jon, shaking with genuine mirth when the mare filled the night with her loud snoring. And Maggie prayed, remembering the Catholic prayers she'd learned as a girl and making up her own prayers, more like conversation with God who, she decided, might be there after all. Maybe no one has proven God exists, but neither has anyone proven God doesn't exist, and it felt good to talk with God, especially about her feelings about Matthew. Maybe she was just talking to herself, but don't they say God is within us? She thought. She imagined herself discussing this with Matthew.

CHAPTER TWENTY-EIGHT

Just before the pre-dawn sky began to lighten, Maggie gave herself over to some much-needed sleep. When she woke, the sun was just peering over the hazy horizon. The smoke was still thick but seemed no worse than it had been the night before. That could be because the wind was flat. She could neither see nor hear any sign of fire nearby. It looked like it would be safe to backtrack to the shallows, cross the creek, and get onto the road that led to Alta Lake. She'd made the right decision last night.

She groaned as she pushed herself up from the unforgiving ground, moving away from Jon who was rolled into an oblivious little bundle, facing toward her. She lifted her gaze and settled on what she had hoped to see—Narnia calmly munching grass in the little clearing next to the creek. Okay God, she thought, so far, so good. Then she felt a stab of urgency to leave this place and get across the creek.

"Hey Jon-O," she said softly, tousling his sleep hair. "Someone is waiting to say good morning, and I think she wants an apple."

Well before sunrise the base camp was in full operation again, and firefighters would soon be deployed in the air as well as on the ground. Ted was in control, barking orders, and Father Matthew and Lucas were taking orders from Jimmy in the field kitchen. They were all excruciatingly aware that Maggie had not called in, but they focused on the business at hand and kept their anxiety to themselves.

Ted strode up to the field kitchen canopy with Jon's parents and Ruthie in tow. Penny Pointer had arrived in a state of hysteria after hearing a local radio station report the fire had engulfed the campground during the night. Ted assured the Pointers that Maggie and Jon were miles from the campground before it caught fire. He turned the family over to Lucas and Father Matthew whose clerical collar, he hoped, would soothe Penny.

"Okay now, I don't have time to answer to each of you separately, so stick together and the minute we hear from Maggie, you'll all find out at once." Ted turned to leave and then beckoned Father Matthew to follow him. Moments later he returned to where the Pointers stood.

"How about some breakfast?" he asked, relying on good scriptural authority that breaking bread together always helps in a tight situation. "We're turning out flapjacks this morning. Grab a plate."

"And when you've finished, maybe you'd like to help out. We have a gazillion sandwiches to make," Lucas added. "I bet you'd like to taste test the brownies after breakfast," he said to Ruthie who seemed to be very interested in the job.

Lucas, Evan and Penny pushed the images of a raging inferno bearing down on their loved ones deep enough into their quaking hearts to keep the panic reflex at bay. But it would have been more difficult if they'd heard the news Ted shared with Father Matthew.

"Father, please pray that Maggie got across that creek. We're sending everything we've got in because the wind has reversed itself and when it picks up it'll be pushing the fire right up the creek in the direction I sent Maggie last night. And that'll be soon."

Father Matthew resigned himself to waiting, the longest wait he had ever experienced.

Maggie put the supplies and the equipment back in the truck while Jon was occupied with giving Narnia her breakfast apple. She heard the first helicopter and knew it was bringing fire retardant. A breeze had begun to swell. The fire was moving toward them. She called Jon and was relieved to see Narnia following him back to the truck.

"In you go, Jon." She stood by the open passenger door, willing him to move fast without her having to alarm him.

"But I'm hungry, Maggie. Where's our picnic blanket?"

"No time for that, Jon-O," she said and nudged him up into the truck.

"And I need to pee."

Maggie realized she had the same need. "Me too, Jon, but we'll have to wait."

The truck started up on the first try. Thank you, God, Maggie whispered. She put it into gear and turned around in their campsite. One mile, she reminded herself, back to that crossing. Please, she whispered as she prayed the shallows would be apparent in daylight. Jon's feet were resting on the silver tent which she'd kept accessible, just in case.

Jon complained about having to go to the bathroom and being hungry, but she tuned it all out as she concentrated. Eight tenths, nine tenths, one mile—the odometer eased over the target up to another tenth of a mile. Maggie's heart was racing along with her mind, reviewing procedure if they were overrun by the fire. Then she saw it.

"Oh my God!" she shouted as she cranked the steering wheel to the left and drove onto the little spit of land that led into the stream bed, with another spit on the other side that signaled this was, indeed, the crossing.

Maggie was between tears and laughter as the truck rolled onto dry ground, and then she became aware that Jon was crying and calling, "Narnia! Narnia!" Oh, no! She realized she had not once thought of the horse since they'd left their campsite, and she held her breath as she stopped the truck. She ran to open Jon's door, and she was crying, too. Narnia was nowhere to be seen.

"Oh Jon, I'm so sorry," she wept as she hugged him to her. She drew in some deep breaths and composed herself. "I'll tell you what. Let's go to the bathroom and then we'll go to the stream and call her. We'll take another apple. I'll bet she just needs to catch up with us."

Standing at the water's edge, Jon called and Maggie strained for a glimpse of the horse through the smoke haze, as if straining would make it happen. She didn't see the horse, but she did see airplanes dropping fire retardant, and she knew smoke jumpers had landed across the creek. The wind was blowing, and although they were safe for now, they had to get back in the truck and make haste toward Alta Lake. She explained to Jon why they'd had to leave so quickly and why they had to leave now. It was hard to explain without frightening him, but he finally turned toward the truck, still calling "Narnia" through his sobs.

Maggie stopped to pull the last brownies out of the food pack and give them to the heartbroken little boy. She started the truck and put it into gear. As the truck began to roll she looked in the rear view mirror out of habit, and through the grey haze she saw the mare in midstream, heading for the bank.

"Our lady's with us, Jon. Let's go."

CHAPTER TWENTY-NINE

The call went through and Ted answered. "Maggie!!" he shouted. "Thank God! Where are you?"

"Up a tree," she answered.

Ted's relief turned to annoyance. "Look, Maggie, we've all been up a tree, wondering if you and the little kid were still alive."

"We're both fine. Jon's a great little trouper. And I mean it—I had to climb a tree to get a phone signal. Good thing I found a spur kit in the cargo box."

Ted approached the field kitchen. His broad smile told the Pointers, Lucas and Father Matthew this was the phone call they'd been praying for. Penny ran toward him, shouting "Jon! Jon! Are you there, baby?"

Ted heard the laughter in Maggie's voice as she said, "Tell Penny I'd put Jon on the phone, but he's about fifty feet below me." She looked down at the little boy standing at the base of the lodge pole pine she was clinging to. She waved the phone. "Your mom says hi," she shouted.

"Where are you, exactly, Maggie?"

"We're at Alta Lake, where the road makes a ninety degree turn to the west."

"What can we do for you?"

"Send out a stock trailer and let me talk to my brother if he's there." Her voice broke against the tension that was dissolving with the promise of help on its way.

"Wait a minute--send out *what*?" Ted turned his head to look at the phone, as if he wondered if it was working right.

"A stock trailer. A mare followed us out. She needs a ride."

"I'll see what I can do," he said. Rolling his eyes upward, he handed the phone to Lucas.

"Where are you? Are you all right? Is the little boy with you? What do you need? Man, am I glad to hear your voice."

"You haven't given me a chance to say anything yet," Maggie laughed. "I need someone to rescue me. I have Jon and we have a horse. Ted's going to find a stock trailer for her. Could someone drive it up here?"

"I'm not sure I could, but Father Matthew might be able to."

Maggie caught her breath. "Father Matthew is there?"

Lucas heard the message in the subtle gasp and handed the phone to the priest.

"I'm here, Maggie," he said.

The sound of his voice brought a flood of emotions she could ill afford at the moment. She choked back tears and blurted the only thing she could think of to say within the bounds of propriety. "Can you haul a horse trailer?"

Father Matthew burst into laughter, startling the group gathered around him. "Yes, I can. No problem." He continued to laugh as she explained the situation, including her precarious position wrapped around the trunk of a pine tree.

"We'll get directions and be there as soon as we can. Just relax and stay put," he said.

"Would you mind praying me down off this tree?" she asked.

"I'll get right on it,," he grinned. "See you soon, Maggie." Father Matthew gave the phone back to Lucas and turned to Ted. "Give me five minutes, and then where do we find a truck and a horse trailer?"

Maggie said goodbye to Lucas and put the phone back in her jacket pocket. Then she rested her head against the tree and the tears began to flow.

CHAPTER THIRTY

"The truck and trailer will be ready in 15 minutes," Ted announced. "Pick 'em up at the sheriff's office."

Sheriff Andy Parker was a genial man who looked tired beyond endurance. His wiry grey hair sprang out from under a hat that sat skewed on his head. He scrutinized Lucas with a look that said he bet the kid didn't know how to haul a trailer.

Lucas introduced himself and Father Matthew. Reading the sheriff's mind, he said, "Father Matthew will drive. He's driven big rigs in the Iraqi desert."

The sheriff nodded, obviously relieved. "Glad you can do the job, Father. I can't spare any of my deputies. We don't usually let people use our equipment, but this is a situation where I can bend the rules. I need a copy of your driver's license."

Father Matthew pulled his wallet from his pocket and took out the license, handing it over. "Is there a halter and lead in the trailer?"

"Yep, and I put a bale of hay in the front compartment. You might need it to entice her into the trailer. I expect she's hungry."

Sheriff Parker stood back and watched Father Matthew start the one-ton. It purred. He grinned at the sheriff.

"Piece o' cake!" He waved as he pulled out, Lucas chugging along behind in his beater half-ton.

Back at the base camp, Lucas picked up enough food to last four people for a week and then he poured coffee into a giant thermos. Ted made sure their mobile phone worked and sent them on their way.

The road was rough, but the truck and trailer, with Matthew's skilled driving, navigated it well. Within an hour they were approaching Alta Lake, but as they crested a hill Father Matthew slammed on the brakes, sending Lucas forward into the dash. "Jesus Christ!" Lucas shouted, and then gulped, far more concerned about his gaffe than about the damage to his forehead.

Father Matthew turned to Lucas and chuckled, his eyes twinkling. "You're okay," he announced and then he pointed toward the gigantic downed alder in front of them, its canopy splayed out over the road. The men got out of the cab and surveyed the problem. "Do we have an axe or a chain saw?" Father Matthew asked.

"Don't think so. Maybe Maggie has an axe in her truck. I'll call her, but unless she's still up that tree it probably won't do any good."

Miraculously, Maggie answered on the first ring. "I have a Pulaski. That should work. I'll be right there." Maggie called for Jon and the horse. "Jon, load up. Narnia's ride is down the road."

As they waited, Father Matthew turned the rig around in preparation for loading up the vagrant horse. The second Maggie's truck appeared, Lucas bolted and weaved his way through the tree limbs. Father Matthew leaned against the truck, giving Lucas a moment with his sister. He watched Maggie open the truck door and when her feet hit the ground Lucas wrapped her in an unreserved bear hug. The priest nodded in appreciation of how close these siblings were.

"I've been worried sick, Mags," Lucas said, his voice thick with emotion. He held her at arm's length. "You look like you fought the fire single-handedly. You're a mess."

Maggie grinned through grateful tears at her brother and said, "Nothing that a bubble bath and a glass of wine won't fix. Oh, yes, and 24 hours of sleep in a feather bed."

She felt a small hand on her left elbow. Remembering her little lost charge, she put her arm around Jon's shoulder and said, "Jon, I'd like you to meet my brother, Lucas, and that's my friend, Father Matthew, over there, on the other side of that tree." She flashed a smile at Matthew and waved.

Looking up through eyes that were red-rimmed from smoke, Jon said, "Hi. Is that a trailer for Narnia so she doesn't have to walk anymore?" Lucas nodded.

Jon smiled and said, "Good. I love Narnia."

"She's a good old girl," Maggie said.

"Why doesn't she walk off?" Lucas whispered when he realized the horse wasn't actually tied to anything.

"I think we've become her herd," Maggie whispered back and they both laughed.

Father Matthew found his way through the alder branches and walked toward Maggie and Jon. "I'm pretty happy to see you two, and who's our surprise guest, here?" He turned to Narnia.

Jon stepped up to introduce the horse. "This is Narnia. She's going to be my horse, well I hope so anyway, but I have to ask my mom and dad." He stopped abruptly and frowned. "Where are they?"

Father Matthew heard the sudden distress in the little boy's voice. "They're waiting for you with your sister back at the firefighters' camp, Jon," He knelt down. "They wanted to come, but the road was too rough for their car, and all of us couldn't fit in the truck."

Maggie was touched by the priest's gentleness. "Well!" she said, bringing attention back to the problem at hand. "Thank you guys for coming to our rescue, but we're not really rescued until this tree is out of the way."

Minutes later the priest was swinging the blade end of the Pulaski into the alder and Lucas was dragging severed branches off the road. It did not escape Maggie's attention that Father Matthew's muscular build looked good in well-worn jeans and a t-shirt.

Soon Maggie was able to guide her truck through. On the other side of the tree, Maggie pulled over and got out, happy to have the two men there to share the responsibility of both the stray horse and Jon.

"I know what we need," Lucas announced. "Come on, Jon, you can help me get the sandwiches."

"Ugh, more roast beef?" Jon grumbled and he shuffled off with Lucas.

"Naw, peanut butter and jelly," Lucas answered and Maggie laughed to see Jon's pace quicken. "Oh boy," she heard him say.

She and Father Matthew stood beside the truck. She said, without looking at him directly, "I'm sorry about Lucas making you think the worst. I hope he didn't ask you to drive all the way over here. I told him to call you if something happened because I didn't want you to think I'd given up on all our work if I didn't show up again."

"No. He didn't ask me to come. I came because you'd gone into a burning forest and they'd lost communication with you. I needed to be here, Maggie." He looked down at her smudged face with undeniable affection.

Maggie shifted uneasily. "Well, Father, I'm glad you're here and I'm really glad you know how to swing an axe," she said, forcing herself back to her old flippancy. "I don't think I could have man-handled that Pulaski at this point."

Lucas and Jon hauled the food pack and thermos to the back of the pickup and set it out on the tailgate. "It's a picnic," Jon cried, clapping his hands. "And there are Snickerdoodles!"

Maggie stepped up to the tailgate. She picked up one of the wrapped sandwiches and held it out. "Here you go, Father," she said.

They all sat in the long grass beside the road, Jon between Maggie and Father Matthew. The little boy tugged on Maggie's sleeve and jerked his head toward the priest. "Is he your father?"

"Huh?" Maggie puzzled.

"You just called him 'Father,'" the boy reminded her.

The adults burst into laughter and Jon's face clouded over. The priest put his arm around Jon's shoulders to explain. "No, Jon, I most certainly am not Maggie's father. She calls me that because I'm a Catholic priest—you know, a preacher—and in the Catholic Church, priests are called 'Father.'"

Jon blinked up at the priest a few times and carefully scrutinized him. "Well, okay, but I know what a preacher is and you don't look much like one to me."

Maggie and Lucas managed to choke back their laughter.

"Hmm," Father Matthew mused. He pulled the knitted neckband of his tee shirt aside and tugged on a thin leather strip that lay under it. A simple wooden cross hung from it. "How's that?" He winked an eye at Jon.

"That's better." Jon turned his attention to his peanut butter and jelly sandwich, and the adults let their laughter escape.

Lucas looked at Father Matthew. "I don't think I understand, either. You look too young to be a priest. Were you ordained at three or am I just used to old men in flowing robes, not a young guy swinging an axe?"

"Actually, age five. I was a slow learner." They all laughed. Lucas noticed a small cross tattooed on the inside of Father Matthew's arm and it made him wonder about the priest's previous life, but he didn't think he knew him well enough to ask. No matter. He would get the scoop from Maggie later. They seemed to know each other surprisingly well for the short time since they'd met.

Lucas asked Maggie if she thought she'd gotten a story for Mr. Stanley out of the ordeal. Maggie smiled as she thought of her boss, a good man whom she respected.

"It might not be the story I was after, but we certainly have a tale to tell. I may have to write about survival with a boy and a horse," she smiled. "And as much as I hate to break up this party, I think we need to see if this horse knows how to trailer."

With some cooperative effort, they managed to halter the horse and attach a lead rope. But it was Jon who performed the most important act of getting her up the ramp and into the trailer. He stood in the front compartment with the hay bale, grabbed a flake, held out his hand, and urged her to come forward.

"Come on, Narnia. Don't be afraid. We're saving you from the fire. I'm going to ask my mom and dad if we can keep you. Would you like that? We might have to move because we don't have a very big back yard, but I know my mom and dad will figure out something."

Narnia's eyes bulged white, but she walked up the ramp and Maggie and Father Matthew pulled the ramp up after her and locked it. As directed, Jon attached the lead to the hook on the side of the trailer, then popped out the side door, a grin splitting his happy face.

"You are a horse whisperer," Father Matthew said. "I never expected her to go in without a fight."

"To tell you the truth, I didn't expect it either," Maggie agreed. "She must be somebody's well trained pet." She frowned, thinking of Jon's devastation if they found that someone, who would surely want her back. But she was just too tired to think about that now.

Seeing his sister's fatigue, Lucas said, "Maggie, load up and let's get out of here. Gimme the keys. You're too tired. I'll drive your rig back, and you can keep Father Matthew company. Jon can ride with me."

She tossed him the keys, her expression radiating gratitude.

Maggie retrieved the versatile fire jacket and climbed into the sheriff's truck. She folded the jacket into a pillow and said to Father Matthew, "If you don't mind, I think I'll sleep. I hope I don't snore." She was instantly asleep and much too tired to snore.

CHAPTER THIRTY-ONE

At base camp, Father Matthew pulled in to a cheering crowd led by Ted.

"Ya got 'em?" he yelled. "Where's the little boy?"

Father Matthew hauled his long frame out of the truck. "Jon is with Lucas in the other truck and Maggie is asleep in here. She's beat."

A new cheer rose up and Ted's face broke into a huge grin as he loped in the direction of the truck that was pulling into the compound. "We gotta get this boy to his folks. The mother's a mess for worrying about him." He waved Lucas toward him. The truck rolled to a stop and Jon was out the door in an instant.

Running toward each other, arms outstretched, Jon and his parents connected in a tangle of kisses and tears. Ruthie scrambled out of her father's arms, to add her hugs. The onlookers moved away. They had observed the safe return, and there was work to be done.

When the crying eased up, the first thing out of Jon's mouth was, "Can I keep Narnia? Can I? Can I?" He wriggled out of his parents' embrace. "Can I?"

Penny's shoulders drooped. "Oh Jon, I don't think—," she started to say, but she couldn't say the words that would extinguish the child's hope.

Evan bent low, to look into Jon's eyes, which were starting to tear up. "There are a lot of things to think about before we can make a decision like that, Jon."

"We could get a new house, maybe a farm," Jon pleaded. "I promise to do all the work."

"I think we need to go home now," his father said, taking his little boy's smudgy hand. "Your friends will take Narnia to a nice place where she'll be happy."

Jon's sobs subsided only when Evan promised they would come back to see Narnia soon. "It's time to say goodbye to Maggie, Lucas and Father Matthew and thank them for their help, son."

As Jon turned toward the trailer where the two men stood, he saw the truck door open and a very unsteady Maggie lowered her feet to the ground.

"Maggie!" Jon shouted and ran to her, nearly knocking her off balance with his bear hug, her second of the day. "Dad says we can think about it, and we can come and visit Narnia, and maybe we can visit you, too and you'll take Narnia someplace nice, and I love Narnia, and I love you, and I'm glad we didn't burn up in the fire—"

Maggie held Jon tightly until the barrage tapered off. "I love you, too, Jon, and I'm sure I'll see you soon." She turned him in the direction of Lucas and Father Matthew.

Jon ran to them. When he had hugged everyone, Maggie stepped to the trailer and opened the side door to let Jon say his last—and most important goodbye. She gave him a boost up into the trailer.

The horse lowered her head to nuzzle the boy. "Narnia, I will always love you," Jon whispered. "I hope I get to keep you and I can learn to ride. I'll figure out where you can live. Be good, Narnia and don't make anybody mad so they want to get rid of you." The horse whickered softly in reply.

Father Matthew joined Maggie at the side door. "Time to go, Jon," he called. He lifted the child out of the trailer and squatted down so as to be his size. "Jon, I want to thank you for taking care of Maggie and Narnia. They both needed your help." Jon reached over and hugged the priest around the neck, then quickly stepped back not sure he should have done that. Tears spilled down Jon's cheeks as the three adults walked him to the Pointers' SUV, where his family waited.

Jon's father stepped forward to face Maggie. "I know it's redundant to thank you again, but we're forever grateful to you. We'll be in touch regarding the horse."

Jon's little hand was still waving out the window as the SUV made its way out of the camp and onto the highway.

They all turned in the direction of Ted. Lucas was the first to speak. "What do we do with this horse?"

"One of the deputies has a horse ranch down the road from here and he'll take her until we find out where she belongs."

"What a lucky lady she is," Lucas observed. "Where is this place? We'll take her on out."

"Easy to find." Ted handed the directions to Lucas and turned away to get back to work. One crisis resolved; others pending.

Lucas jumped in his truck and yelled, "I'll lead this time."

Back in the truck, headed toward Narnia's new refuge, Maggie rested her head against the door. As he drove, Father Matthew glanced at her, beautiful in repose, despite the dirt and grime. Her eyes opened, "I wonder if Jon's getting anywhere with his parents about keeping Narnia," she murmured.

Father Matthew chuckled. "Probably driving them nuts. Perhaps we could make a deal with the ranch owner to take care of her so Jon can come to see her on weekends."

"Hmmm," was all she said before her eyelids closed.

Thirty minutes later that's exactly what they did.

CHAPTER THIRTY-TWO

Back in the parking area of the base camp, Lucas wrapped Maggie in her third bear hug of the day. "Mags, I hope you realize you scared the holy shit—sorry Father—out of me. I'm too young for that kind of stress so I'm heading back to Seattle to drink a beer and recuperate."

"Lucas, you're the best. Thanks for coming over." She returned her brother's hug and said, "I'm not sure your old crate will make another trip over the pass, but, if it dies, I owe you a rescue. Tell Mom I'm fine and I'm going back to Spokane." She didn't notice Father Matthew's grin widen at the news. "I'll call and let her know how things unfold."

Lucas turned to Father Matthew and the two men shook hands warmly. "It's been fun, Father. Hope we cross paths again when the smoke isn't so thick. Watch out for Maggie. She's a handful."

Lucas climbed into his truck, waved and was off. Turning back to the base camp, Maggie and Father Matthew noticed a group of people surrounding Ted.

Maggie saw his back before she saw his face or heard his words. She froze. The man turned around, a surly look on his bearded face. "So there you are!" he shouted. "What the hell did you think you were doing out there? You had the entire office in an uproar. You were sent over here to gather statistics and get field information for the Forest Service. We didn't send you out on a goddamn rescue mission. This nonsense could cost you your job." Walking toward Maggie, he sneered. "You don't get paid to save little boys and old horses. You're paid to write articles about disasters."

"Who the hell are you?" Father Matthew asked, the curse word rolling off his tongue easily, his years in the oil fields showing in his defensive stance.

"I'm her boss and she needs to get off her ass and do her job".

"Hold on there, fella," Ted joined in. "You have a strange way of showing concern about an employee." Ted's large body, hardened by years of field work, towered over the other man's desk-softened frame. "This lady not only saved a child and a horse, she insured the safety of five other people. Put that in your report."

Recovering her composure, Maggie stepped forward and glared at Bruce. "You most certainly are *not* my boss, Bruce. I don't work for you now and I won't ever work for you. I work for Mr. Stanley, and he'll have my report as soon as I write it." She drew a deep breath. "You worry about your own ass and I'll take care of mine."

Bruce bristled at the put-down by a woman in front of a gathering of men. He raised a clenched fist.

Father Matthew stepped between the bully and Maggie. "I think it's time for you to leave."

Father Matthew saw Ted reach inside his jacket pocket and grasp something, perhaps a wrench, something he was sure could lay Bruce cold.

"Who are you?" Bruce spit it out in a pointless attempt to intimidate the man facing him. "Let me guess. Maggie's new best friend." His sarcasm hung in the air.

"Matthew Brannigan's the name."

"Oh yeah--you're the priest. Now what are you doing out here? You and God saving her? Where's your black bathrobe?" he mocked.

Father Matthew stepped forward until he was eye to eye with the man. "You can leave on your own two feet, or you can leave in an ambulance. Your choice."

Bruce took a step backward and looked past Father Matthew. "What about you, Maggie? You coming back?"

"I'm afraid not."

"You owe us a statistical report. If you don't come back with me now, I'll see to it you're fired and you don't ever get another job." It was a futile attempt to salvage a shred of self-respect. His voice whined in the midst of the tough, seasoned firefighters.

"You're too late," she said. "I've accepted another job."

Bruce backed up. "I can't believe you did that. You owe me. You can't just walk out." He sputtered in frustration. "Think how long we've worked together."

Maggie clenched her fists. "I owe you nothing. Not one single thing, you arrogant prick." She looked to see Father Matthew gape-jawed in astonishment "Sorry, Father."

A faint smile flickered across his face. Father Matthew cocked his head and shrugged his shoulders as if to say, "What's left to say after that?"

At that, Maggie's rage dissolved and her old charming self was back. "C'mon, Father Matthew, let's go solve some problems. I have all the time in the world. As soon as I get a hot meal I want to get back to Spokane so we can wrap up the Curious Case of Great-aunt Milly." She strode through the group of men, toward the food tent.

Once again, Father Matthew Brannigan simply shrugged his broad shoulders and smiled.

CHAPTER THIRTY-THREE

Jimmy's smile brightened the whole food tent. "Miss Callahan, we're mighty pleased to be feeding you this afternoon," he said in greeting. "Give me five minutes and I'll give you the best Croque Monsieur you ever ate. You too, Father Matthew."

"You're on, Jimmy. And I know for a fact there's some rhubarb pie for dessert." Turning to Maggie, he whispered, "I made it."

Properly impressed, Maggie nodded her head. Father Matthew guided her to one of the tables and they slid into the benches, facing each other. They sat in comfortable silence, savoring the first moments of quiet peace either had experienced in two days.

"Another job, eh?" the priest finally asked, his eyes riveting hers.

"You might call it self-employed," Maggie answered without making eye contact, having been caught in a slight exaggeration of the truth. "I've wanted to try freelancing for a long time, and I can go where I please—anywhere I can drive or a plane can fly me."

The priest grinned. "That sounds like you, Maggie. And how will your boss take the news?"

Maggie frowned. "Oh, damn—"she darted an apologetic glance, as if he had never heard a curse word nor used one just recently. "I suppose Bruce has already called Mr. Stanley. I need to call him as soon as I get back to my mobile phone. Mr. Stanley is a good man. I think he'll be one of my best customers."

"Yeah, I need to call my boss, too," Matthew said as Jimmy put the hot sandwiches in front of them.

After the meal, which included a generous slice of the best rhubarb pie Maggie had ever eaten, they walked to her car to pick up a change of clothes and a towel she had filched from her B and B. "I plan to return it," she replied defiantly to Father Matthew's snicker.

She picked up the mobile phone where she'd left it earlier to charge in its case. "I might as well get this over with," she sighed.

She was heartened by Mr. Stanley's response to the news. "You're one in a million, Maggie. I wish you luck," he had said.

"Any more juice in that phone?" Father Matthew asked when she finished her call.

"Of course!" She handed over the phone and left the priest to deal with the bishop on his own. On her way to the field shower she noticed a man seated at one of the tables. Strange to see anyone sitting down around here, she thought. He wore a windbreaker zipped up, tight around his neck, also strange on a hot afternoon.

Bishop Davis picked up on the first ring. "What do you think you're doing?" he shouted.

"Watching out for Miss Callahan, your eminence," Matthew answered, "as you instructed."

"Is she coming back to Spokane?" he demanded.

"I believe she is, Eminence."

"When will you be back?"

Matthew scratched his fingernail back and forth across the mouthpiece. "What is that again?"

"When will you be back here?" the bishop shouted, louder.

"Sorry, sir, could you repeat that?" Matthew tapped the transmitter rapidly. He heard the bishop say, "What's wrong with your blasted phone?" and then Matthew broke the connection.

His second call was to Father Francesco to let him know he and Maggie would be resuming the search for answers—but not immediately.

CHAPTER THIRTY-FOUR

They walked to Maggie's car. Father Matthew stopped and said, "Before we get going, I have a suggestion."

"What?"

"You've just been through an exhausting couple of days, and I have to admit I found them a little trying too. Let's take the long route back to Spokane. We can drive up to Lake Pateros, grab a boat, maybe some fishing poles, and hang out on one of Washington State's prettiest lakes. We might even get lucky and hook a walleye if you're agreeable to the detour and a mini holiday."

It took Maggie less than a second to consider the offer. "You bet I'm agreeable. I'd love to do that."

Father Matthew opened the passenger door with a gallant flourish. "Miss Callahan, I am at your service."

She climbed in and they drove out of the base camp with Father Matthew at the wheel.

As soon as they were underway, Father Matthew turned the air conditioner on high and rolled down the windows. "We're going to let the smell of smoke and the stress of the last few days blow out of the car and we are going to forget about life as we presently know it. "

A thrill of anticipation mixed with a hint of danger coursed through Maggie. She shivered and said, "Bring it on!"

They drove as fast as Highway 2 would allow, then turned onto Route 97. Father Matthew slowed to a comfortable speed and Maggie sank into the seat beside him. She rode with her eyes closed. Eventually she said, "Won't the bishop wonder why you're not on your way back to Grand Coulee?"

"I'm sure he will, but I am doing exactly what he told me to do. I am looking out for you." Father Matthew grinned. "Besides we're heading there. We're just not taking the most direct route."

"I don't get it. You appear to take his orders, yet I sense you challenging him. Doesn't the vow of obedience get tangled up in there somehow?"

Father Matthew darted a glance at her, as if to assess whether it was a question that wanted answering. "I try to do what he asks but I do it the way that fits how I see a priest doing it. I like to think of myself as a pastoral priest. In order to keep in touch with my flock, I need to go where they are even if it means I have to meet them at a pub for a beer or at a baseball game or, sometimes even, at a forest fire."

Maggie nodded, encouraging him to go on.

"I don't think the Church should wait for people to come to it. It's my responsibility to go where their lives are. That's how we keep the Church alive. I minister to them on their turf. I go to kids' sports events, golf courses, the Moose Club, PTA meetings, service organizations, pinochle parties. I minister to the elderly who wait for me to come and sit with them for an hour or so. I like to think they live a little longer and a little better because they know I really care about them. They think I have a direct connection to God, and maybe that gives them some level of comfort as they draw closer to meeting Him. I'm fairly easy to get along with. Maybe that's why the bishop picked me to follow you around."

"You are easy to get along with, but that sounds way too perfect. No flaws in the armor?"

"Oh, I have flaws. I just try to keep them under wraps."

Maggie digested all he had said for a few moments then asked, "What would you have done if you hadn't become a priest? Did you always want to be a priest?"

"I've always had a healthy respect for God and the Church, but I came to the priesthood late. I didn't enjoy working in the oil fields. I liked the idea of caring for a parish more than driving big rigs in a hot desert. There was little humanity connected with that job."

Maggie leaned back against the headrest, and let the air blow against her face. "You never wanted kids or a family?"

"Never met anyone that might have led me in that direction, I guess. How about you?"

"Nope. I haven't either. Not yet anyway. I could never wrap my head around the idea of marriage and kids. I really like kids, and if I ever meet a good daddy for them, I might have one or two. But I also love my career."

"You can't have both marriage and a career?"

The irony of hearing that from a Catholic priest struck her, but she resisted making a point of it and went on. "I would need someone with similar interests to mine. Someone who would go study the coral reefs in Australia or go to Central America to count butterflies, someone who would be willing to climb Mt. St. Helens just to look into an active crater. That person would also have to like the arts and want to go to the theater or see a good movie or visit an art or science museum. This probably sounds crazy, but I want to live a life of contagious joy, and anyone I was linked to would have to feel that way too. And, of course, someone who likes to read. I guess I'm waiting for some kind of a contemporary Renaissance man."

Father Matthew considered what she had described, then said, "Speaking of reading, have you read the Book of Acts? That's its message. Live a life that brings you joy. It all sounds like a reasonable aspiration."

They approached a turn in the road with a broad view of the valley. Father Matthew pulled off the road. "Let's take a picture of this. I have a camera in my duffel bag."

Maggie got out and sprinted across the road. "Gorgeous. How many views like this have I missed by riding with my eyes closed?"

"No more than ten," Father Matthew laughed. "By the way, I phoned ahead and reserved a couple of rooms at the resort. I wanted to be sure we had a place to stay. There is no way we want to drive the last part of this road in the dark. We'd miss too many picturesque pot holes." Maggie looked at him and grinned, but didn't say a word.

They climbed down the hill a few feet and stood on a large flat rock that jutted out. Maggie said, "This valley is so beautiful it takes my breath away." They stood side by side in silence absorbing the splendor of the high mountain desert below.

It was Maggie who broke the spell. "Shall we go? I don't want to miss any more spectacular views."

"Your wish is my command." Maggie groaned at the cliché and they climbed back up the hill. Father Matthew bowed as he opened her door.

The sun had slipped behind the treetops in its long, leisurely Northwest descent when they reached Lake Pateros. Maggie paid for her room. She wasn't going to be obligated to Father Matthew or his church. She wondered if Father Matthew had used his title or just registered under his own name. She hadn't noticed any raised eyebrows so he must have omitted the 'Fr'. They agreed to go for a walk and then have dinner.

The air was pleasantly cool after the heat of the August day. They walked in silence savoring the smells and the noises of the evening. Crickets, night hawks, a breeze through the trees, the occasional grumble of a Great Blue Heron.

The mood was interrupted by Father Matthew. "Tomorrow morning we fish. That means we're on the lake by six. Once it warms up, the fish don't bite. This is strictly a catch and release expedition, you understand."

"Okay by me. That means breakfast about five. Hope the kitchen is open."

Father Matthew laughed. "Always thinking about food. How about a compromise—muffins and coffee at five-thirty?"

Her room was tiny. A twin bed, a table and chair, a small closet and a no-nonsense bathroom. No TV but they did provide an ancient clock radio. Not dissimilar to Father Matthew's room back in Grand Coulee, Maggie imagined.

She popped open her bag and pulled out the navy blue silk blouse she'd stuck in on a whim. The silk blouse and clean jeans would have to do. She pulled the iron and ironing board from the closet, set it up, turned the heat on to medium and pressed out the wrinkles. Why am I going to all this trouble? She wondered. Remember, Mary Margaret Callahan, as much as you might like it, this is not a date.

When she arrived at the restaurant, Father Matthew was waiting, dressed in clean jeans and a dark shirt *sans* clerical collar. "Let's eat outside. Is that all right with you?"

"Absolutely. The sunset should be spectacular."

They found a table with a view of the lake and sat side by side so both could watch the action on the water. After they ordered Father Matthew twisted slightly in his chair and asked, "So, Maggie, what would you do if you weren't chasing disasters?"

Maggie answered immediately. "I'd be writing something—not sure what, but the world revolves around story, you know. I have a friend in Seattle who writes humor. Her latest project is a collection of bizarre stories about people's weddings. You'd be amazed at what people tell her. One couple came out of their wedding reception smiling and happy, ready to leave for their honeymoon, to find no car waiting for them. Someone had stolen it, cans tied to the bumper and all. The first thing they did as a married couple was to go to the jail house to file a stolen car report. Someone got them to the airport on time, with a police escort."

Matthew laughed. "Did they find the car?"

"Days later. But the worst part was that their luggage was in the stolen car, so they left on their honeymoon with not much more than the clothes on their backs."

Maggie's laughter captivated the people trying not to eavesdrop. Father Matthew smiled, enjoying the company of his animated dinner partner. This was definitely an uncommon occurrence in the life of a priest.

The apple pie was served with dark espresso coffee. They watched the sun go down and felt night close in. It had been a delightful day.

Maggie rose at 5:00 AM, dressed in a tee-shirt under her long-sleeved flannel shirt and pulled on her jeans. She slathered her face and ears with sunscreen, grabbed her old visor hat and walked to the lobby. In addition to helping herself to rolls and coffee, she stuffed apples and bananas into her bag, always preparing for what might come.

Wondering where Father Matthew might be, she stepped out on the prodigious wooden porch and saw him on the dock. He waved and motioned for her to come down. Fishing poles rested on the center seat of a rowboat tied to the piling. He knelt to hold the little boat steady against the dock and smiled at her, but said nothing more than "Get in." Once settled, he rowed silently, the oars barely skimming the water. Maggie lay back in the boat and gazed at the sky and the mountains. Life could not be more ideal than at this moment.

Father Matthew broke into her reverie. "It's time to fish. I bought worms. Do I need to bait your hook?" She could see he was chagrined the second he asked the question.

"I suspect you already know the answer to that. When I was a kid, Dad took Lucas and me fishing a lot. I had to bait the hooks because Dad was busy with the boat and Lucas was too little. Besides, he hated to kill those slimy, worms. Maybe that's why he wants to become a doctor—he hates to kill anything."

"I like your brother. I was impressed that he needed to be there when you came out of the fire. During our short time together, all he talked about was what a great sister you are. Not the typical behavior of a sibling. I asked him what he thought made both of you so quick to help other people. He said he knew I wanted him to say it was church influence, but instead he said it was your father."

Maggie nodded. "Mom provided the dos and don'ts of good behavior, but it was Dad who introduced us to the wonders of the world." Tears were close; her loss was still raw.

"You miss your father." The priest's voice was soft.

"I do. I know he died with something on his heart he'd meant to tell me. I think finding out what it was is the last thing I can do for him. Everything points me to learn the truth about Aunt Milly." Maggie wiped her eyes on the sleeve of her flannel shirt.

Father Matthew cast his line into the water, and it immediately pulled taut. "Fish on!" he exclaimed. He pulled the line up to the boat, grabbed a small net, and pulled the fish in. It was a nice sized perch. "I hate to throw this guy back. Nothing better than a perch fried in butter with lots of salt and pepper."

He gently released the fish, rebaited his hook and said, "What would you like to do in your spare time, assuming you have spare time?"

Maggie thought about it, holding her pole slack. "Let's see. I'd like to see the world. I love a good rodeo. I like to garden. I'm seventy-five percent an outdoors person and twenty-five percent townie. Oh, and I'd like to work on a dude ranch. But mostly, I'd like to travel and then write about it. Now you, Father. What would you like to do?"

"Well, the world interests me, too. I always wanted to get a small motor home and work at all the national parks, a few months in each. I figured I could help people along the way and see the country. Then I'd do the same thing in Europe and the Middle East and then I'd go to Australia and Asia last. Before I entered the priesthood, I actually considered doing it," he said with a hint of wistfulness in his voice.

"Couldn't you do this and still be a priest? Be sort of an itinerant padre? You know. Have Collar. Will Travel." She laughed, quite amused with herself.

"Maggie, you're mocking me again. It doesn't work that way and you know it. I'd want to share that type of travel with someone other than some guy whose idea of haute couture is black."

Maggie laughed out loud and thought, this guy has a great sense of humor— for a clergyman.

As the sun rose higher in the sky, the lake warmed. Maggie and Father Matthew removed their long-sleeved shirts and Maggie spotted the Celtic cross tattoo. In a bold move, she leaned forward and touched it.

"I felt I needed to make a statement—one the roughnecks in the oil fields would understand. Had a devil of a time finding a tattoo artist who would do it. Too close to proselytizing, I guess. I finally found a closet Christian to do it, and we got to be friends."

"I like it," she murmured.

The fish ceased to bite. "Time to head for shore and back to Grand Coulee." Father Matthew reeled in his line. "Why don't you keep trolling on the way back? You never know what you might catch." Father Matthew rowed slowly across still waters. This had been an idyllic morning.

As Maggie wrestled her suitcase over the threshold into the lobby, she heard the desk clerk say, "Thank you for staying with us, Father." Ah, he did use his title, she thought, but when she looked up the man was not Father Matthew. A shorter man in a windbreaker stood at the desk, his back to her. As he left she did not see his face, and when Father Matthew came in moments later, she forgot to tell him about the coincidence.

CHAPTER THIRTY-FIVE

The drive back to Grand Coulee was slow. Maggie put her arms behind her head and stretched out. "What would you do if you could do anything to help mankind?"

"Easy—I would design a machine that could distill sewage gray water into potable water."

"I'm impressed! But don't we already have that?" Maggie said.

"Yes, for cities but not for individuals. I'm talking about something every human being around the globe could have at a price lower than dirt."

Maggie looked at him with interest. That didn't sound like something taught in a seminary. "Is this a dream? Could you figure out a way to do it?"

Matthew smiled at her across the car. "It's my utopian dream. Think of how we could improve global health and save lives if everyone had access to clean water. I'd like to put my engineering degree to use working on it."

"I thought you were a truck driver."

Matthew smiled. "It's true—I drove big rigs in the Middle East. But my real job was supervising the oil restoration operations. It was easy to give that up for the priesthood."

"Do you know anything about geology?" Maggie asked.

"I'm supposed to," he answered. "I'm a geological engineer."

"So you must be aware that all these pot holes were formed about ten or twelve thousand years ago." Maggie's tone touched on supercilious.

Father Matthew gazed at the landscape and said he didn't know about that.

"Well, let me explain," she said, a mischievous smirk playing about her face. "When the ice age began to melt, mammoth sheets of ice flowed south out of Canada and piled up to create an enormous ice dam where Missoula, Montana is now. So water from the Clark River and the glacial melt filled up behind the dam until it was over half a mile deep, and—"

"I bet the dam failed," Father Matthew interrupted, "and water raced across the country at fifty or sixty miles per hour and dug out the coulee we know as 'Grand Coulee.'"

"And, uh, left these scars we call potholes…" She was crestfallen. "You're making fun of me," she said.

"Not a bit. It's a fascinating world we live in, Miss Maggie Callahan, and I really didn't know about the potholes. Seeing it is a lot better than reading about it, and hearing about it from you is better yet."

She brightened. "And I suppose all this could have happened by what they call 'the hand of God,'" she conceded. He smiled at her and nodded and turned his attention back to the pock-marked road.

They soaked up the rugged beauty of the Eastern Washington terrain until Maggie asked, "How did you come to the parish in Grand Coulee?"

"Priests are sent to where they're needed, as it matches their training. I served as an assistant to Bishop Davis. That was right out of seminary. Then the bishop appointed me to the Saint Francis parish. I am still officially his assistant."

Maggie snickered, "Once an altar boy always an altar boy."

Father Matthew smiled at her puckish sense of humor. "I'm afraid so when you're a lowly parish priest. We serve at the pleasure of the bishop." He broke off, and Maggie sensed his relationship with the bishop was disappointing to him.

Changing the subject, he said, "By the way, why do you have a spur attached to your rear view mirror?" Father Matthew noted the leather was brittle from age, but the rowel still spun when wind blew through the open windows of the car.

Maggie reached up and gave the old rowel a whirl. "It belonged to Milly's husband—Great-uncle Ben. Milly told Dad to give it to one of his kids, so now I have it, and it's with me wherever I go. Guess I'll give it to one of my kids someday. If I, uh, have any, that is."

They drove the last leg of the journey in silence. Father Matthew's thoughts churned. They had spent time together, separated from the lives and people they knew. They'd had fun like he had never experienced before. His head knew to turn his thoughts elsewhere, but his heart couldn't help wondering what a future with Maggie would be like.

Nearing Grand Coulee, Maggie asked to pull over at the crest of a hill. Looking at the desert below, she said, "That valley is so beautiful."

"And so are you." Father Matthew said it so softly she couldn't be sure she heard him correctly. Then he drew a deep breath and turned to Maggie. "I have something to tell you," he said, and the spell was broken.

Her eyes widened as she heard about Prudence Pittock's letter. "So there *is* evidence of some impropriety," she said. "But how do we learn the priest's name, and what came of it, and whether it had anything to do with my Aunt Milly?"

"I can't answer that, but I spoke with Father Francesco after I called the bishop, and he suggested he would have a surprise for us if you returned."

"As if a pride of snarling lions could keep me away," she said.

CHAPTER THIRTY-SIX

Father Francesco stood before the bishop, as erect as his old body would allow.

"They know, don't they?" the bishop roared.

"What is it they are not supposed to know, Eminence?" This conversation was going to be very trying for the old priest.

"You have stolen the key to the private archives. I know because it was not with the rest of the keys when you returned them. What have you found? What do they know? Tell me." Father Francesco had never heard such fury in the bishop's voice.

"Eminence, I have nothing to tell you other than what you already know," Father Francesco said, truthfully. His soft voice never wavered, but nearly imperceptible tremors tugged at his face.

The bishop stomped around his desk and stood face to face with the old priest. He hissed, "Remember carefully. You took a vow of poverty, chastity, and obedience. You are not obeying my demand to tell me what you found in the archives and what you have told that prying woman."

"Eminence, you know the documents I removed from their file. And I have told Miss Callahan nothing." Father Francesco wondered how long he could withstand the bishop's badgering or whether a bolt of lightning would strike him dead for his sin of omission.

The bishop growled through his teeth. "Get out of here. Get out before I take action I might live to regret."

Father Francesco turned and walked from the room breathing a sigh of relief that in his fit of anger, the bishop had forgotten to ask for the key. He scuffled to his cottage and fell into his favorite chair, pondering what might come of his actions. History, he thought, isn't always pretty, but it must not be denied. *Ego me absolvo*, he whispered to himself.

CHAPTER THIRTY-SEVEN

Father Francesco opened the door, and with outstretched arms welcomed Maggie and Father Matthew. "I have cleaned the house in your honor," he chuckled. Gazing around the room, all they could see were piles that had been shifted and restacked. He had made a gallant effort, but it was really a hopeless cause.

"I understand you are the heroine of the day, Maggie. Father Matthew told me about the boy and the horse. I admire your spunk, to say nothing of your cool head in a time of extreme danger. Father Matthew, you are in charge of tea. It's brewing. I bought cookies for the occasion. Please put them on a plate."

Father Matthew did as he was bid, taking a moment to see if the envelope was still there and if there was anything new. Nothing. He returned to the living room with the tea tray and raisin-oatmeal cookies.

Maggie waited apprehensively for the old priest to say something, but he remained silent. She stared at the two priests. What were they waiting for?

Father Francesco sipped his tea. "Now, as to my position paper for Rome."

"I'm sorry Father," Maggie broke in, "I thought you had something to tell us about my search. Is that not true?"

"Oh my. Oh my. You're so right. I forgot." He feigned innocence as he pushed himself off his chair and stood. He reached into his robe and then pulled out the prize. "I believe this may lead you to what you want to know. Our incensed bishop accused me of stealing the key to the private archives, something I would never do. Fortunately he was so angry he forgot to ask me to give it back." Father Francesco's face broke into an impish grin.

"Will the bishop discipline you?" Father Matthew asked, concerned about the risk he knew the old priest had taken.

"Perhaps, but as someone—maybe Shakespeare—said, 'The deed must be done now or not done at all.' We shall do our deed in the wee hours, say at one-thirty? The campus should be sound asleep by then."

Father Francesco replaced the archaic key and settled back into his chair. "Ah, now let's get on with it. I've written a first draft and I look forward to revising it with fresh perspective after our conversation. Because we are mature people, I feel we can discuss questions of sex as an academic exercise without personalizing it, thus not making any one of us uncomfortable."

He sneaked a peek, looking for a reaction. Seeing none, he went on. "Here are the ground rules for our discussion. I want you to raise questions about celibacy as it relates to the priesthood. Then I want your frank opinions. I expect that you will have questions and theories that I've not thought of. Father Matthew, please take the point of view of the Church. Maggie, you take the lay point of view. I hope that among the three of us we can cover all the questions anyone might want to direct toward the Church."

Maggie fidgeted with her napkin, distracted by the prospect of what might be unearthed in the forbidden archives. "I can do this but I feel a little out of place. Are you sure you want me in this discussion?"

"I do. Your viewpoint is fresh and, better yet, from the female perspective. Two priests simply support what we already know. You don't." Father Francesco was emphatic..

"I'll try." She took a deep breath. Tomorrow would have to wait until tomorrow. "I'm ready."

Father Francesco beamed his pleasure. "The first point of discussion deals with the notion that celibacy within ranks of the clergy is a significant problem that the Church must defend. My question is why."

Father Matthew spoke first. "I think you must first address the fact that celibacy is canon law. It is not absolute law. I am assuming you have introduced the history of celibacy and the clergy in your paper and we don't have to go over it here."

"I have. I discuss the third, sixth and seventeenth centuries when celibacy was officially reaffirmed by the Church as a religious value. Although other churches—most notably, the Eastern Orthodox Church—have elected to allow priests to marry, the Roman Catholic Church has not. The assumption is Jesus never married. Priests are the embodiment of Jesus, therefore, priests should never marry."

Maggie entered in. "Poppycock! That speculation began when the Church was trying to pull away from female dominated religion. I believe by the time the third century rolled around, they'd managed to make celibacy the moral code."

"Partly true," said Father Matthew. "But there was also an economic issue. If Church wealth supported priests' families, it would not be Church wealth anymore and priests' worldly goods would be handed down to their next of kin, not the Church. So the Vatican said priests must devote all their time to their parishes and, like Jesus, do their work among the faithful, unencumbered by worldly impediments such as wives and offspring. And estates."

Maggie jumped in. "But look at the gospel of Mary, the mother of Jesus. Although it was not included in the New Testament, it speaks of the need for family. Apparently Mary thought a family was important to the well-being of the men who carried Jesus's message. That would be in keeping with the Jewish mores of the time. And Jesus was a Jew."

Father Francesco dumped three cubes of sugar in his tea and looked around with a guilty smile. "No wonder I am so fat." Stirring his tea vigorously to dissolve the sugar, he went on. "The modern Church also believes that having celibate priests means having no worries about pregnancies, abortions, breakups, divorces or STDs. In other words, the Church does not have to worry about social headaches within its clergy."

Maggie pointed out the irony that parish priests are expected to deal with these problems on a daily basis. "How can they answer questions about which they know very little? They have no first-hand information."

Father Matthew quickly answered as the Church might speak. "There are myriad subjects about which a person can be knowledgeable without first-hand information. Scientists who know about big bangs and quarks and galaxies haven't traveled out there, but they can extrapolate information from study and they can deal with abstract ideas. So it follows that priests can be reasonably wise about social institutions and dilemmas involved in marriage, divorce, children, birth control, and so on without going there themselves."

"The fallacy in your argument, Father Matthew, is that scientists and mathematicians are dealing with absolutes. They come up with only one right answer, even if there are varied ways to get there. It's a world of black and white. Priests, on the other hand, are dealing with people, where there are only shades of gray. There are as many answers to questions dealing with the social issues you refer to as there are people who experience them, and unless you've walked a mile in their moccasins, you can't truly know what it's all about."

Father Francesco held up his hands, palms out, facing his two guests. "Whoa there. I need to digest some of this." He began to scribble on his lined pad.

Maggie blinked. "I can't stop now," she erupted. "Why does the Church assume celibacy keeps any form of sex from happening? We all know about priests who carry on affairs. How do you answer that? Sex is a very natural and necessary part of the animal kingdom of which we are members, like it or not." She tossed her head and blew back a rash of curls that had fallen forward over her eyebrows.

Maggie glanced at the two priests, wondering if she had gone too far with her candidness, but she plowed ahead. "The Church only condones sex for the purpose of procreation, otherwise it's a sin. What nonsense. Most people would like to dump the stigma of original sin and just enjoy the sex."

The two priests stared at her. Father Francesco's pencil was stilled, and she saw Father Matthew stifle a smile. She crossed her arms and delivered her final salvo.

"While we're at it, tell me why women can't be priests." She leaned back in her chair and picked up her teacup. "Now it's your turn."

Father Francesco coughed and Father Matthew cleared his throat, but neither spoke. Finally Matthew broke the impasse. "The simple and truthful answer is because the Church is a patriarchal society and the Vatican isn't ready to make that change."

"You are so right," Maggie's eyes narrowed and she spoke through clenched teeth. "The Church supports the point of view that women are lesser than men because woman was formed from Adam's rib. And then Eve led Adam down the primrose path with the apple incident, and for that little transgression she got to bear the babies in pain and suffering. Whoop-de-do!"

Father Matthew blew out his breath. "If women were ordained, there could be a power struggle and the Church doesn't want to deal with problems that would surface between males and females—the same kind of competition issues that arise in the lay world." He hesitated before going on. "But mostly, men don't want to give up the right to be the final decision-maker. There is that unspoken need to keep women in their place." Father Matthew realized he was taking on Maggie's message, and he wondered how that happened.

Maggie's smile bordered on smugness. "My point, exactly. It's time the Church moved out of the dark ages. The Church still has to deal with priests unfaithful to their vows, gay priests, and abusive priests, not to mention nuns who leave the Church to give birth or to marry. A few women in the clergy might get these sticky situations sorted out."

Father Francesco was taking notes at lightning speed. When he looked up, Maggie was sure she would be asked to leave. Instead, she saw his eyes, merry in the presence of passion and new ideas.

"I hear what you're saying," he said, "but we'll leave gender issues for the next position paper. He put his lined pad and pencil on the stack of books serving as a side table. "I'd like to finish up by asking you a personal question, if you don't mind, Maggie. Would you marry a priest if it were allowed?"

Maggie turned away from the old priest's bullet gaze and stared at the wall, noticing for the first time that Father Francesco's homey little cottage was in serious need of paint, and the stacks of books and journals were leaning into bookcases which lined the walls. Her mind raced. How could she answer this question with Father Matthew sitting across from her?

She took a deep breath. "If it were allowed, I could and I would. But under today's rules there would have to be a love so profound that not marrying would be an unbearable loss."

Father Matthew rose and went to the kitchen to recharge the teapot. He wondered how long Maggie had thought about these questions. She was articulate. Had she been in love with a priest? Research, he thought. After all she is a journalist.

When Father Matthew returned with the final round of freshly brewed tea, he delivered the part of the argument he had begun to grapple with days before this conversation began. It was from point of view of the Church, but not what Maggie or Father Francesco might have expected.

"The Second Vatican Council in the 1960s deemed that celibacy *wasn't* compulsory, but that it was appropriate," he began. "That's contradictory to what the Church has proclaimed as law for the last two thousand years. If the Vatican Council publicly said that celibacy is optional, then why is it even an issue with the Church? Do you know if any priest has ever challenged this statement by asking to marry and remain a priest?"

"Yes, in South America and some European countries," Father Francesco conceded. "Perhaps some in North America, but I've not followed that question until recently. I must make it a point to find out before I submit this paper." He made a note on the lined pad.

The old man winced as he stood to stretch. "I think that is enough for now. You two are kind, to indulge an old man. Such good questions. Such thought provoking observations. I am grateful to both of you." He made the sign of the cross over each of them. "Now, Maggie, you must go home and get some rest. Father Matthew will call you in the morning."

As they left, Father Francesco patted Matthew's shoulder. "I will see you later, my boy. You may have to wake me."

CHAPTER THIRTY-EIGHT

At half past one the Holy Names campus was quiet. Father Matthew knocked lightly on Father Francesco's door wondering if he had fallen asleep after they had left. The door opened to Father Francesco standing in the dark. "Come in, come in," he whispered. He turned and motioned for Matthew to follow. Speaking softly he said, "This is how I think this should work. We'll stroll toward the church. If anyone is awake and sees us, we can tell them I have trouble sleeping. They'll believe it because I'm an old man. You had been at my cottage helping me with my paper and said we should go for a walk because maybe the night air would help me sleep. Or do you have a better idea?"

"Nope. Sounds good to me."

"Good. When we get there, you will go down the stairs, into the private archives.

"But Father—" Matthew began to protest.

"No, no," the old priest countered the protest. "The stairs are too hard on my knees. I will keep watch."

"But where will I start? How can I hope to cover several years of documents in the time we have?"

"You might start with 1940."

"But that is beyond the time frame we've been given. Would it make more sense to—?"

"I suggest you start with 1940," was the firm answer. "Now let's not talk. We might attract the attention of some other poor insomniac who is out walking at this absurd hour."

They both chuckled and began a slow stroll toward the church, Father Francesco bent over, occasionally stopping to rest. Father Matthew held tight to his arm.

Once in the archival museum, the two groped their way to the stairway in silence. Father Francesco put the key to the iron door into Matthew's hand and pulled a small headlamp from the folds of his robe, pointing to the bottom of the stairs where it would be safe to turn it on. Matthew nodded.

Once down the stairs, the young priest turned on the headlamp and wrestled with the obsolete lock and the heavy door. Nervous about turning on a light, he walked around the perimeter shelves, shining the headlamp on the labels until he found the one marked 1940. He groaned when he saw the box was stuffed to the bursting point. But before he began to pull the first folders out to begin a methodical search, he noticed a conspicuous green file in the middle of the box. It stood slightly higher than the others and carried a 1936 label. Misfiled. He tugged on it until it pulled away from the jam.

From what he could see by the light of his headlamp, Father Matthew knew he had found what he was looking for. He removed the document, shoved the folder back into the box, and put the box back into its slot on the shelf. It had taken him less than five minutes.

With the purloined paper folded and safely tucked into his pocket, Father Matthew relocked the door by headlamp light and then climbed the stairs in the dark. He and Father Francesco retraced their route in darkness and in silence, leaving nothing behind to tell of their furtive excursion.

Once back in the cottage, Father Francesco checked to be certain the window shades were pulled, then turned on a lamp. It would be easy to answer why he had a light on past midnight. It would be a continuation of the story about a walk to help him sleep. He sank into a chair and said, "I'm too old for much more of this clandestine work even though it's quite exhilarating. I am exhausted."

Father Matthew took the document out of his pocket and unfolded it. He held it out to the old priest who waved it away. "No, no, I'm much too tired to read anything. Just tell me what it says."

"It is addressed to Pope Pius XI, by way of Bishop Ryan, from a priest who is asking for a release from his vows. He says he has been drawn toward a worldly life and must choose between that and his love for the Church and the Holy Orders. He says his request is long overdue, and he begs His Holiness's indulgence and compassion in granting the release." Father Matthew looked up from the sheet of paper in his hand. "I can almost feel the anguish of the man who wrote it."

"Yes," Father Francesco murmured. "I know." His eyes glistened with tears that were close to spilling over.

"The name is not redacted—Father Anthony deMarco. I believe I recognize it."

Father Francesco's eyebrows lifted. "Is that so?" he said as if he were surprised.

"Yes. He is one of the elderly priests I have visited at the monastery."

"Ah," said Father Francesco with a sigh of relief. "Perhaps you should pay him another visit, and take the young lady with you."

CHAPTER THIRTY-NINE

Bishop Davis parked in front of St. Ignatius Care Center and gazed at the ivy covering the monastery's rock walls. He hated to talk with Father Anthony, but felt it necessary for the good of the mother Church. He was sure Maggie would find Anthony soon, and he had to have the old man prepared to deny everything.

The ivy's waxy, hunter green leaves created an inviting setting. He wished he could just sit beneath the wall and pray for a little while. At times such as these, he felt the full weight of his position and his past decisions.

He reflected on what he would say to Father Anthony. He had to be delicate, but firm. If the old priest was going to tell the young woman everything, he, as the head of the diocese, had to be prepared for damage to the Spokane church, maybe even the entire diocese, especially himself. A scandal in his diocese would not be accepted well by the Cardinal.. He felt somewhat guilty that he could not remember the last time he had come to the monastery or spoken to the aging priests who resided there.

In the dining room he stopped to exchange pleasantries with several of the elderly priests, asking how they were getting along and if they were provided with everything they needed. The men stared at him, some wondering who he was, others wondering why their bishop had abandoned them. Turning to the nun who stood quietly at his side, he said, "Why isn't Father Anthony here with the others?"

"He doesn't venture outside his room much anymore, Bishop Davis. You know he is not doing well. His mind is still very sharp, but his body is failing. He doesn't move away from his room often because he doesn't like to bother anyone by asking for help. They put him in his chair in the morning and again in the afternoon after his nap. He is in his wheel chair now waiting for you. Please don't stay too long, Eminence. He is very weak. I believe his time to meet our Lord is near."

"I see. Does anyone visit him?" The bishop was very grave as he spoke to the attending nun.

"No. Father Matthew Brannigan drops in occasionally to visit all of our residents, but other than that, you are his first outside visitor in over a year. Except for his confessor, of course."

"No family comes to visit?"

"No. Any close family has long since passed, or they've forgotten he is here."

"Thank you, Sister, I'll not stay long." The brief exchange with the nun only intensified his sense of guilt, and he drew a deep breath to regain his composure.

"Please show me to Father Anthony's room now, Sister Mary Amelia." The bishop walked down the drab hall, thinking to himself that the walls should be painted yellow to create a feeling of warmth. When it was his turn to be in this building, he did not want to see hospital grey-green walls.

He stopped a moment in the doorway staring at the back of the man sitting at the window, shoulders hunched and draped with a hospital throw to ward off the air-conditioned chill of the room. Bishop Davis moved across the room, and the old man's head lifted at the sound of footsteps. He smiled when his visitor came into view, and Bishop Davis saw a trace of the vigorous man he had once been.

"Good afternoon, Father Anthony. You look well."

"Thank you. And you as well, Bishop Davis." The old man bowed his head. "Please present your ring. I am unable to rise." In spite of his infirmities, the old priest insisted on following the time-honored traditions of the Church. The bishop presented his hand and Anthony kissed the ring.

Bishop Davis unlocked the brake and turned the wheelchair. He relocked the brake, then pulled the only chair available—a large, avocado-colored plastic armchair—so it faced Father Anthony. The big man sat with a ponderous "whoof" at the effort.

"I'm sorry I haven't come to see you more often. The duties of the office are on-going as you know." He faltered for a moment before going on. "But I'm afraid this isn't just a social call. I'm also here on Church business."

Father Anthony looked with alert, but cloudy eyes at Bishop Davis and said, "Church business? How could Church business involve me after all these years?"

"A young woman from Seattle might come by to speak with you. If she does, she will ask questions about events that may have transpired in the late thirties. She's searching for information about a family member. She thinks something questionable happened but she doesn't know what. She is trying to put some old family rumors to rest. I don't know if she will find you or not, but if she does I am asking you to please spare the Church a scandal."

The old man obviously grasped the situation. "I see."

Bishop Davis studied his ring for a moment. "Of course you can tell her anything you want, but remember whatever you say reflects on the Church." He hoped he had been persuasive.

"I understand." The old priest looked through eyes filling with tears at this man who never came to see him and came now only to deliver a thinly veiled order. "You do not want a scandal. But I've carried the weight of my memories for so long, like an albatross attached to my soul."

"You don't have to tell her anything. Think on it."

"Yes, as I have thought on it every day of my life." He sighed deeply and said, "I'm sure you will be asked to deliver the last rites shortly, Eminence. I feel the end is near. I want to be ready."

"I will come to you when it is time. You will receive the blessed oil."

"Thank you, Eminence. I have one last questions. What does she know already?"

"She believes her great-aunt, Milly, shot a priest." The two men stared at each other, fifty years of silent history hovering between them.

"Please ask Sister Mary Amelia to have the orderlies put me back to bed. I am very tired."

Bishop Davis turned to leave the room and summon the nun. As he reached the door, Father Anthony's voice carried across the room. "And Eminence, I can no longer tolerate blackmail."

The orderlies came and assisted Father Anthony back into bed. They fluffed the pillows, pulled down his bed shirt so it covered his boney legs, then started to pull the light blanket over the old man.

"Please don't cover me. I'm fine for now. I'll call you if I get cold." The orderlies looked with sympathy upon the old man who so often chose discomfort and even suffering, as if to shrive his soul.

Bishop Davis wheeled the Town and Country out of the parking lot, his mind still reeling from the encounter with Father Anthony. Blackmail. He couldn't stop an unconscionable thought. If luck was on his side, the old man would die before Maggie Callahan found him.

CHAPTER FORTY

Maggie pulled out her dark blue silk blouse, which was beginning to feel like a uniform, and a pair of dressy pants. She preferred jeans, but felt they were a bit too casual for meeting the old priest. She grabbed a double shot mocha on the way to the church where she picked up Father Matthew. "I'm a little nervous. I don't know what to expect," she confided.

As they drove, Father Matthew counseled her not to invite stress until they knew what Father Anthony had to say. "You may not learn anything that answers your questions."

"I have a feeling I will. Will you stay with me?"

"I will if you want me to."

Maggie turned to him, fear of the unknown in her expression. "Father, don't ask me where it comes from, but I feel this is the end of the line." She told him of the dream she'd had just hours before, where her grandmother led her through a long series of doors, each becoming larger and brighter, until she was walking toward the light and her grandmother disappeared. He made no comment, but he did not seem critical or dubious.

The sparsely furnished greeting room at the old monastery was nearly empty. Four elderly men sat at a table playing pinochle. A cross hung on one wall and a picture of Jesus hung slightly askew on the opposite wall. One small window framed the garden. Sister Mary Amelia ushered Father Matthew and Maggie past the old men and led the two guests down the dimly lit hallway.

She stopped at the third door. "This is Father Anthony's room. He tires easily, so please do not stay too long."

They entered the small, hospital-drab room. There was a bed, its side rails up, a small chest of drawers, a night stand, a wheel chair and the plastic arm chair where Bishop Davis had sat the day before. Above the bed hung a large wooden cross. A tattered prayer book rested on the nightstand. The pages were once trimmed in gold ink, but that had long been worn away by Father Anthony's daily devotions. There was an aura of age and neglect about the room.

The priest sat up in bed, bolstered by pillows. His eyes were closed, but he opened them as they approached the bed, Maggie in the lead. He startled and choked, an explosive, strangling sound.

Mary Amelia rushed to his side. "Father, shall I call for the doctor?" she asked in alarm. He closed his eyes and shook his head, struggling to calm himself and regain his breath.

Finally he whispered, "So I have guests. Three guests in two days. That must be some kind of record, wouldn't you say Sister Mary Amelia?" He waved the nun away, giving her permission to get on with her duties elsewhere. "Wait, Sister, could you ask an orderly to bring another chair?" He smiled his appreciation, and Maggie saw kindness in his brown-black eyes and the deep lines etched in a face supported by classic Italian bone structure. His hair was still black, with a smattering of silver. This has been a handsome man, she thought.

Sister Mary Amelia returned, folding chair in hand. "Father, please call, if you need anything." She left, eyeing the two visitors, her expression quizzical as if she were wondering what brought Bishop Davis here yesterday after more than a year's absence and now these two. One could believe she might linger outside the door and eavesdrop, but Sister Mary Amelia was not one to give in to such a temptation.

Father Anthony observed the two young people before him and said, "It's good to see you, Father Matthew. Would you care to introduce your friend?"

"May I present Miss Maggie Callahan, from Seattle. Maggie, this is Father Anthony deMarco."

The old priest turned to Maggie and seemed to study her face before he finally said, "So you wish to speak to me, Miss Doyle. Bishop Davis said you might be along."

Formally, as if she were a child asking for an audience with the most important man she knew, Maggie said, "Yes. It's an honor to meet you and I would like to speak to you about my great-aunt, Milly. Mildred Miller was her full name. She lived in Grand Coulee in the early 1930s and in Spokane for a very short time. There are family rumors—I'm trying to find out—well, I'm hoping you can shed some light on what happened. And by the way, my last name is Callahan. Doyle was the maiden name of my great-aunt and her sister, my grandmother."

"Of course. Forgive me, my dear. You see, when you first came in and I opened my eyes, I saw Evangeline Doyle standing before me. It triggered my choking spell. You are the image of your grandmother." He motioned to the two chairs. "Please sit."

Maggie took the folding chair, and Father Matthew placed the arm chair at an angle so he could see Maggie's face. He saw that she was rigid, her body tense. The ancient priest knew her grandmother. It was a promising start. Matthew looked nearly as tense as Maggie.

Father Anthony turned to Matthew. "Father Francesco speaks highly of you."

"What? You know Father Francesco"

"Oh, yes. Father Francesco and I are old friends."

Matthew was speechless, obviously surprised by this information.

Maggie didn't take her eyes off the old man. He knows Father Francesco? Does Francesco know this man knew my grandmother? Why didn't he send me here in the first place? Why all the clandestine machinations?

It was Bishop Anthony who broke the impasse. "How did you find me?"

Maggie started the narrative, "There were family stories about Great-aunt Milly shooting a priest at Grand Coulee. I am using my vacation to find out if it was true. I went to St. Francis Church where I met Father Matthew. He has been helping me." She stared down at her hands, clasped tightly in her lap. Her fingers were bloodless and white.

Father Matthew picked up the story for her. "Maggie came to my church asking to search the records for the period surrounding the alleged shooting. The bishop permitted me to search the church records for her, but to no avail. Then she interviewed an elderly gentleman in my parish who remembered that Mildred Miller had a sister, Evangeline, who lived in Spokane." He turned to Maggie.

Maggie went on. "Since I'd found nothing about Milly's shooting a priest in Grand Coulee, I came to Spokane. The bishop allowed Father Matthew to search the diocese archives for me. Other than that, however, Bishop Davis has stonewalled me at every turn, and I must admit I find it odd."

Matthew nodded his wordless agreement of her assessment.

"I had nearly given up when we found a letter written by a disgruntled Holy Names parishioner complaining about the behavior of one of the priests, but the priest's name had been clipped out. It encouraged us, though to continue the search." Maggie had transitioned from "I" to "we" so seamlessly she didn't even notice, but Father Anthony's mouth quirked into a small smile.

Father Matthew took over the narrative and confirmed his sense of partnership in the effort. "Then, quite by accident, we found another letter in the private diocese archives that was likely related to the first—."

"By accident?" Father Anthony interrupted.

"Yes, I would never have found it, as it had been misfiled, but Father Francesco—." Matthew stopped and his eyes went wide as he remembered how Father Francesco had insisted he search the 1940 files and he understood perfectly why his mentor had manipulated the search. "He is your confessor!"

"Yes, for decades. And I was his bishop."

"His bishop?" Maggie and Father Matthew said in unison. Matthew was visibly discomfited by this news and his failure to observe protocol. "Your Eminence, I apologize—I had no idea."

"That is by design, Father Matthew. I chose to give up the title when I gave up the bishopric. I prefer to be Father Anthony, not Bishop deMarco. It suits my station and my penance. Now, about the letter you found by accident?"

"It was signed by you, Father Anthony," Father Matthew confirmed.

"So you found out I was still alive." He stated it as a fact rather than a question.

"Yes, and that you lived in this monastery," Maggie added.

"And this is where I've lived for over fifty years."

Maggie did a quick calculation. "That would mean you retired in your mid-thirties." She frowned, puzzled.

"I did not retire early. I chose to live here while I conducted my church duties, for reasons you will learn." With long, boney fingers, the priest beckoned them to move their chairs closer. "I am frail and very tired." Maggie sat on the edge of the hard seat, eager to hear his words.

"Miss Callahan," he began, "your great-aunt is not the object of your search. What I am about to tell you I've never told another living soul, except my confessor. Maggie—if I may—I need you to know the truth. It is a story long overdue." His eyes scanned the room as his mind searched for the years when he was a young priest in Spokane so many years ago.

Maggie leaned forward willing him to speak. Father Matthew reached for her hand. Her face earnest, she murmured, "I'm listening."

"I loved your grandmother with all my heart and soul."

The words slammed Maggie back against the chair. "My grandmother? You loved my grandmother?" She was stunned.

"Yes, and I love her still. I loved her more than my obligations to the church." He paused. "No, I guess that's not true or I would have made other choices. But not a day has passed that I haven't paid for my choices in regret and prayed for her forgiveness." He sank into his pillows and seemed to shrink before their eyes

Silence filled the room like a heavy mist. Memories. Questions. Astonishment. More questions. Each churning mind focused on a different piece of the puzzle.

"This will take some time. I am prepared to tell you all, but you must have patience, my child. I must rest now so I have the strength to tell you everything you want to know. Come back tomorrow at one o'clock. I will be rested by then." He looked long at Maggie, seeing the Evangeline of so long ago. His eyes filled with tears. Rather than let Maggie and Father Matthew see them spill over, he turned his head to the wall.

CHAPTER FORTY-ONE

The air was hot and dense when they drove away from the monastery. Thunderclouds darkened the sky. In the distance, heat lightning flashed. It felt and looked like rain. The car was full of silence. Finally Maggie stuck her arm out the window feeling for raindrops and said, "I hope it rains."

"Spokane can always use rain," Matthew said with relief in his voice that her stunned silence was broken. "How about a burger?" They found the ice cream parlor that resembled a 1950s diner and sat at the counter. Maggie said, absentmindedly, "Father, do you think he is telling the truth about my grandmother?"

"I do. I believe this is his last confession."

"His last confession?" She looked sharply at him. "You think he is going to die? I don't want this to be the cause of his death."

"It won't be the cause of his death. I think this is a personal confession, Maggie. God already knows. Father Anthony wants you to know." Father Matthew looked at their reflections in the mirror behind the counter. He noted her unpretentious beauty and how very lost she looked as she grappled with the situation

"Father, do you believe in purgatory?"

"Where did that question come from?" Father Matthew looked at Maggie, searching her face for a clue. "Are you asking if I believe that if I do something bad, I will spend ten thousand years in purgatory? No, I don't believe that."

"But isn't that what we're taught as kids, in the Church?"

"Yes kids learn that if they do not die in a state of grace, there's a stop off in purgatory. Unless they've been so bad they go straight to hell. Scare tactics."

"So what do you believe?"

"I believe we have to atone for what we've done through confession and penance while we're still on earth. The grace we receive right here on earth keeps us out of purgatory—both here and on the other side."

"How about Father Anthony?"

"Are you asking if I think he has atoned for all his sins? I have to say I don't know."

"Well I don't know about the atonement part, but he sinned all right, Father." Her tone was adamant.

"Most likely. Not many among us haven't," he commented philosophically.

Maggie toyed with the straw in her milk shake. "I'm almost afraid to hear any more from him. This much has changed everything I thought I knew about my family. My own grandmother!"

He looked at her sharply. "What? Suddenly, you don't want the truth? You can't stop now. Maggie, I think you've been led here, to this place, to Father Anthony." He paused. "To me."

Abruptly, Maggie changed the subject. "Did you ever have a girlfriend?" Father Matthew looked at her, his deep eyes searching her face. He thought, I'll never totally understand this woman and how her mind works.

"You're really all over the map with your questions today. Yes, I had several girlfriends along the way, but none more serious than a good friend. None ever made me want to take it to the next level."

"Did you ever wish you could find someone who would make you want to take it to the next level?" She was immediately sorry she'd asked the question; she had no right. She held her hand up in a "stop" signal. "You don't have to answer that," she said, and he didn't.

CHAPTER FORTY-TWO

They returned to the monastery, as instructed, at exactly one o'clock. Father Matthew hung back, letting Maggie take the lead, not wanting to interfere but wanting her to know that he was there as her advocate. Sister Mary Amelia met them at the door. She grabbed Maggie's hand and held it.

"I don't know what your business is with Father Anthony, but I want you to know he has suffered greatly."

"And you don't want me to add to his suffering," Maggie finished the thought for her.

"No!" Mary Amelia exclaimed. "What I wanted to say is, I think you may have the power to relieve his suffering."

Maggie searched the nun's eyes hoping for an explanation, but none was forthcoming. The three entered the building. Maggie took a deep breath, and they entered the room.

Father Anthony was in his wheel chair dressed in a black shirt, but no clerical collar. "You're right on time," he smiled. "I slept well last night. Perhaps it is because I am cleansing my conscience."

"And what needs cleansing, Father Anthony?" Maggie asked in her signature direct manner. She leaned forward in the straight back folding chair.

"Patience, child. It will all become quite clear."

"I admit to a lack of patience, Father. Forgive me." Maggie leaned back in the chair and folded her hands as the old man began his story.

"I first saw Evangeline on the Fourth of July, 1935. We were walking in opposite directions through the Holy Names grounds. Her copper red hair caught my eye. We glanced at each other and I nodded to her. I remembered her when we met a few weeks later at an after-Mass potluck. She had come from St. Joseph, Missouri, to be with her sister, Milly, who had moved to Spokane to start a new life. Evangeline had just gotten her first teaching job, and she bubbled over with ideas for her forthcoming classes. I thought her students would be very fortunate, indeed, to have a teacher so animated and full of joy.

"Evangeline was a regular worshipper at Sunday Mass—Milly not so much—and I found myself looking for her and making it a point to speak with her during the coffee hour. Why not? I told myself. She brought a youthful perspective to the Church. I was young, too, albeit eight years older than she. The winter passed pleasantly, the more so because of those Sunday moments with Evangeline—Miss Doyle it was, then.

"Evangeline and her sister were inseparable, so everyone was shocked in the spring when Milly announced she was moving to Idaho. Evangeline scraped up enough money to buy an old station wagon—one of the first, I think—and I helped them pack for the move.. The plan was that during Easter vacation Evangeline would take Milly to the place she'd found on the St. Joe River. Milly was full of plans for fishing and farming.

"I said goodbye to Milly and Evangeline and was dumbstruck by my own sense of loss. I went back to my room and lay on my bed.

I was terrified that Evangeline would never come back. I feared she would fall in love with the St. Joe River and want to stay with her sister.

"When I saw Evangeline's red curls in the back pew on Easter Sunday, I was so relieved I could barely keep my mind focused on the most holy Mass of the Church year."

Maggie glanced at Father Matthew to see if she could read any thoughts into his solemn face. He didn't look at her.

"Did you have more contact with her after that?" Maggie asked, wanting to get on with it.

"It was difficult, but I learned she liked to walk along the path at the River Park in the evening. As the weather warmed up and the days began to lengthen. I managed to get a dispensation to leave the church campus by myself. You see in those days priests were allowed to leave campus only in the company of another priest. But I told Bishop Ryan I wanted to go running in order to keep up my athletic skills. I convinced him the exercise would be good for my soul. The good bishop agreed it might not be fair to another, less athletic priest to have to keep up with me."

"And you chose to run along the path at the River Park," Maggie guessed.

"Of course. At first I would stop when I found her on the path, exchange pleasantries, and then move on. But the pleasantries began to grow into longer conversations, and by summer, when night didn't fall until bedtime, we met as often as possible and walked together, quite openly and for longer periods of time. It was all I could do to focus on my priestly duties each day, as I counted the hours and the minutes until evening prayers were over and I could leave for the River Park. We shared everything about our lives, and I couldn't hear enough about hers—her work, her family, her faith journey. And she seemed interested in mine—my Italian heritage, my preparation for the priesthood, my daily routine.

"The only time I lied was when she asked me how I felt about being a priest. The truth was I loved the richness of the Mass, the ritual, the intellectual stimulation, the service I provided to my flock. It was easy for me to follow the Church's lead, but to Evangeline I said I often felt stifled. But of course I wasn't stifled by the Church; I was stifled by my own feelings about her. At night I lay on my narrow bed and stared at a faded print of Jesus, my mind on Evangeline. I hoped she was as captivated with me as I was with her. When I could stand it no longer, I rolled off the bed onto my knees, opened my breviary, made the sign of the cross, and began prayers. Night after night I did this, but I seldom focused on prayers. I focused on Evangeline. Constantly my prayers wandered away from theology and onto her. I admit I was obsessed with her."

"My confessor reminded me there are sins of thought and sins of deed. He also reminded me of my vows. After confession and penance I felt strong enough to withstand the temptation of Evangeline, but as soon as I saw her, I knew in my heart I wasn't strong. She was my Achilles Heel. I was deeply concerned about not being faithful to my vows. I loved the Church and desperately wanted to be true to my calling, but then there was Evangeline."

"Did she know how you felt?" Maggie asked.

"I couldn't imagine her not knowing, although she never acknowledged it. I remember one Mass when she came forward for Communion. All I could think about was how she smelled of lavender, roses and face talcum. My hands shook as I presented the wafer. If she was aware, she made no response. She walked back to her pew, her eyes down.

"As fall set in and evenings shortened we had less time to spend together, and our walks were less frequent. I tried to see her more at church as she participated in activities, but we were seldom alone. In November Evangeline was to be the attendant at a friend's wedding at which I was officiating. She was changing clothes in one of the small rooms. I walked in on her, not realizing she was there. I just stood there, embarrassed, and then I walked over and kissed the back of her neck, at the nape. Not a word was spoken. Terrified that someone would see me, I left. There was no response from her.

"After that I did not find her on the river path. I rationalized that winter had set in, that it was hard for both of us to get away early enough to walk before darkness fell, that the path could be treacherous when the temperature fell below freezing. I saw her at Mass and served communion to her, but she was not joining the congregation in the parish hall after Mass. I was desolate."

Maggie interrupted. "Did it occur to you that she admired you as a priest and didn't dare admit to any other feelings she might have about you?"

"Yes, that occurred to me, and for her sake I went no further in expressing my feelings for her. I managed to get through the Christmas Holy Days and began to run again, this time farther from the cathedral, in Minnehaha Park where I could pick and choose my trails. One afternoon in the early spring I rounded a curve on one of the less traveled trails and saw her ahead of me. It was as if all those empty weeks had dissolved. We sat on an old bench made out of a log and visited until the sun set. We both knew I could not accept her offer of a ride back to the cathedral, so we walked to her car in the darkness and said good night.

"I fully expected her to tell me we couldn't do this again, so I was not prepared for what happened next. But that will have to wait. I am tired." The old priest closed his eyes and asked them to call for Sister Mary Amelia. "Come again tomorrow at one o'clock," he said.

Maggie led Father Matthew out of the room. "I see something coming that he may not want to be honest about."

"I think you're wrong Maggie. The end is near for him. I think he wants to set the story straight, tell you everything. I think every word of this is true."

CHAPTER FORTY-THREE

The afternoon had warmed up to ninety-five degrees. "In your robes?" Maggie exclaimed when she picked up Father Mathew. He put a handsome tooled leather case in the back seat and assured her the robe was summer weight wash and wear. They arrived back at the monastery and found the old priest lying in his bed, his head slightly elevated, his arms resting on the sheet that neatly covered his wasted frame. He smiled when they entered the room. He seemed comfortable, eager to continue his story.

"Thank you, my dear, for indulging an old man. Let's see, where were we?"

Maggie wanted to sigh, but knew she would have to control her impatience. She smiled and offered him her hand which he held as he went on with his story.

"Oh, yes, we had met in Minnehaha Park and I was overjoyed to be with her again. But at the next Sunday Mass, I missed her in the congregation. I was beside myself. After Mass, I was stopped by an elderly parishioner who wanted to talk about Sunday School classes. She didn't feel the children were getting enough religion. I listened out of one ear, always watching for Evangeline. Finally the woman became agitated because I was so distracted. 'Father, your mind is elsewhere. I will talk to you later when I have your attention.' She never showed up, and I learned she wrote a letter instead, complaining that my behavior should be investigated, as she suspected conduct unbecoming a priest. She was right, of course, but Bishop Ryan merely warned me gently to avoid such criticism, and he certainly didn't send the letter on to the pope as she expected."

Maggie and Matthew connected a glance; that was the letter with the name redacted.

"I was frantic when Evangeline was nowhere to be seen at church for the next two weeks, nor on any of the trails we'd hiked together. Later in the month I met her in Minnehaha Park, sitting on the wooden bench where we had met before. Perhaps she had been waiting. I couldn't help wondering how the timing had been so perfect. She smiled at me and motioned for me to sit beside her.

"She seemed nervous. 'I like to walk,' she said. I can hear her voice now. Like musical notes. 'This trail is my favorite. There is so much beauty to behold.'

"She made small talk about the wildlife she enjoyed in the park. She brought bread for the squirrels, but told me Milly would disapprove if she knew she was feeding the wildlife.

"Finally Evangeline searched my face and asked me to tell her what I had planned for my life. Did I plan to move up in the Church? I was honest. 'Eventually, yes, I believe I'm being prepared for a higher position.' She did not respond.

"We walked to a rock stairway that led to the river. When we reached the last two steps, we had to climb over blackberry vines. I jumped, then beckoned her to jump. 'I'll catch you,' I said to her. Evangeline jumped and landed in my arms. She made no attempt to release herself from my embrace, but, rather, she clung to me. Gasping, her face ablaze, she finally eased herself free and patted down her clothes. I let her go and stepped back. Neither of us said a word. We continued along the river bank, she picking up flat rocks, skipping them across the water, and me challenging my mind to stop thinking about what just happened. It was awkward. I tried to take her hand, but she pulled away and I let her go."

The room was silent. Finally Maggie spoke. "Was it still an obsession, or had you truly fallen in love with my grandmother?"

"It was love, my dear, pure and undeniable. And unbearable. Back in my room all I could think about was how she had felt in my arms. I wondered if I could become her confessor. Then we could talk without people knowing. What would we say to each other within the walls of the confessional? I wanted to hold her, caress her face, and touch her lips, not things done in a confessional. I would scream at myself inwardly, 'Stop! You have no right to go on this way.' For days I forced myself to stay away from the paths where we might meet, but I could not bear not seeing her.

"The following Sunday, Evangeline attended early Mass. Dressed in black, she sat in the last pew. I saw her and could barely control my shaking hands. She saw me and smiled in an innocent sort of way. She did not come forward for communion, but left before the end of the Mass.

"That evening, after prayers, I made my run to Minnehaha Park. I was sitting on a rock gazing south over the valley. The Spokane River was visible in the distance. I saw her and rose to greet her. I touched her hand to see if she would pull away and I told her I had thought of little except her.

"She closed her eyes and began to weep. 'Oh Father, and I of you. I struggle not to think about you, but it's a losing struggle.'

"I did not let go of her hand. I whispered that I wanted, only, to be with her. Then she asked me, 'What does that mean? Are you saying you love me? Would you leave the priesthood?'

"I didn't answer until she pulled her hand away. 'Yes, if you care for me as I care for you.'

"She held very still as I softly kissed her. Then I pulled her into my arms and the kiss became passionate. Pulling away, breathless, she said, 'Oh Father, we must be careful. We don't want to be seen. I do care, more than you can imagine, but please know I will not be merely your mistress.' She said it with such conviction I believed her, and she believed me when I said, 'My love for you is true. I will never hurt you.'

"Then she told me she was caretaking a friend's house for two weeks. She gave me the address and told me to come after dark, through the alley. She said the door would be open. She walked away and did not look back.

"We made love every night until the approaching dawn forced me to return to my own bed where I would pray for forgiveness and guidance until it was time to prepare for my day as a priest. We promised eternal devotion. I wrote the required letter to the pope asking to be released from my vows so we could marry. I read it to her and promised to deliver it to the bishop who would endorse it and send it on to the pope. She said she would continue teaching, knowing it would take time to work through Church bureaucracy. And we reminded each other of the disastrous consequences if anyone learned about us. I assured her all would be well, that our love was pure in God's eyes.

"The last night of our fortnight tryst, Evangeline asked me to meet her at our special bench in Minnehaha Park the next Tuesday. 'I have a plan,' she said.

"The nights without her were an agony. We didn't speak after Mass, terrified it would be too easy for others to see how we felt about each other. Finally Tuesday came, and I met her at the wooden bench. We sat together and watched the river, not knowing what to say. Finally she asked me to walk with her and she led me to a rustic little stone building that was secluded in the underbrush, well off the main path. Inside was a cot, clean and in good repair. A quilt was folded on top of it, and Evangeline shook it out to cover the cot.

"'I will come here every Tuesday at dusk,' she said. "I will wait half an hour. If you don't arrive, I will know you were detained, and I will return home.' She must have seen my surprise, for she fell into my arms and wept as I held her. She said, 'Oh, forgive me, Father. I know exactly what I do.' Then we lay on the quilt and made love."

Maggie's face was unreadable, paralyzed by this accounting of her beloved grandmother. It was as sad and desperate a story as she had ever heard. "Go on, Father Anthony."

"We lived separate lives, except on Tuesdays and Sundays. Spring became summer. My heart was breaking because I had not yet fulfilled my promise. Every waking hour I struggled with my conscience. I would prostrate myself before Jesus and renounce Evangeline. As soon as I finished, I would think about her and how I could not give her up. I knew I was a hypocrite, going about my priestly duties. When incense wafted during Mass, I thought it was Evangeline's perfume filling my senses.

"As August waned and the new school term approached, she lowered her eyes one evening after our lovemaking and asked, 'What do you want from me?' I told her I wanted to marry her, to have a life with her. It was true, but what she said next was also true.

"'Father, I want this as much as you do, but I am so afraid for you and me. The Church is the third person in this relationship.' Then she looked directly into my eyes and asked me when the pope might respond to my letter. I could not return her gaze. 'Bishop Ryan never sent it,' I admitted.

"What I didn't admit was the long conversation the bishop and I had engaged in, how he had told me I would surely be the next bishop, how he had promised me I would have a glorious future in the Church if I didn't succumb to my weakness of the flesh" The old priest began to sob. "How, God help me, I withdrew my request."

As if he were reliving the awful past, the old man lay sobbing, helpless to stem the tears pouring past his temples and control the convulsive spasms that wracked his frail body. Maggie wanted to scream at this man for what he had done, but pity for his suffering held back her angry words. She really wanted to know what it was her father wanted to tell her as he lay dying.

CHAPTER FORTY-FOUR

Father Matthew and Maggie called for Sister Mary Amelia and then stepped out of the old priest's room to let him recover from his emotional surge. They went to the atrium which had once been a screened porch for summer sleeping. The few potted plants in residence were turning yellow with neglect and lack of water. Matthew and Maggie sat side by side in wicker chairs which were, no doubt, relics from the early days of the sleeping porch.

Tears began to roll down Maggie's cheeks, tears of frustration and sorrow that she'd never be able to talk about these revelations with her father. And Father Anthony hadn't even reached the part about a shooting, if, indeed there had been one.

Father Matthew took her hand. His touch rocketed through her, but she didn't move her hand away.

"Are you okay?"

Maggie's answer was full of embarrassed nervous tension. "I don't know how to respond. I came asking for family history, but I didn't expect to learn my grandmother had an affair with a priest. A pretty lurid one, at that. Did you know about any of this?

"No, I didn't know."

"Did the bishop know?"

"He tells me, no, but—"

"You don't believe him."

"No, I don't believe him. He called me in this morning and demanded to know what Father Anthony had told us. I told him the truth, but I had a strong feeling it's something else he fears."

The temperature had hit triple digits by the time Sister Mary Amelia came to say Father Anthony was composed and rested. Maggie again sat at his side.

The old priest lay still in his bed, Maggie could see his thoughts were far away. Finally he spoke. "I want to go back to my own education. It was pounded into us when we reached teen years that sex was only for married couples. We were not to engage in sexual activity of any kind. Celibacy was pounded into us even before we entered the seminary. I strayed."

"Father, we know you strayed. You had sex. That, in itself, is not scandalous. Or shouldn't be, anyway. Are we talking about celibacy as a priest?" Maggie moved her chair closer to the priest so she could watch his reactions.

"I'd rather say we are talking about love."

"But you failed to leave the priesthood for love. You left my grandmother alone with her shame. How can you say it was love, now?"

"It was very difficult. Very difficult," he rambled, biding time until he was able to go on with the story. He heaved a great sigh.

"Evangeline did not ask why my letter had not been sent to the pope, and I'll never know if I could have explained it. She disappeared from my life and I grieved the loss more than if she had died. Indeed, it felt like I had killed her.

"Then, at the end of 1936 I became the center of attention. Bishop Ryan, who had convinced me to withdraw my letter to the Vatican, passed away of a massive heart attack. His death was so sudden and unexpected it cast the entire diocese into turmoil. I had been led to believe I was the heir apparent, but I assumed the Vatican would find someone older to fill the bishopric. Instead, I was sent to the Vatican to study. I was overjoyed and stunned a few months later when I learned I was to be the new bishop. I met Pope Pius XI briefly, then headed home with the understanding that I would continue to study. I traveled to diocese headquarters in great cities around the country and entered into a life I could never have dreamed of.

"There were no more thoughts of Evangeline. If my past entered my mind at all, I rationalized that I had been chosen to sacrifice for the overall good of the Church. I saw myself as a martyr, and I thanked God for it. By the time I was installed as bishop, it was 1937.

"The next few years, for me, were very good. I was good at my job and well thought of throughout the diocese. Other dioceses even sought my assistance in training young priests to future leadership roles.

"Then one day my young assistant, Father John, came to me with a problem. 'Eminence,' he said, 'there is a woman who is asking that her child be baptized.' He told me he had asked the woman why she hadn't baptized the child as an infant. She admitted she was not married and could not identify the father. Then he asked why she wanted the child baptized now, and she said the child was very ill and might die soon. He explained to her that we could not baptize the child because the child was illegitimate and because she, the mother was not a member of Holy Names. He said the woman wept and said she would go to other churches until she found someone to baptize her daughter. Father John explained it was unlikely that anyone would honor her wishes.

"I told him he had handled the situation correctly, and then I sent the priest back to his duties. He was a good assistant, smart, devoted to the Church.

"A week later Father John came to say the woman was back, this time with the child, who did appear to be gravely ill, and she insisted upon discussing the issue with the bishop. She refused to leave until she had seen me. I said I would see her.

"I opened the door. She stood there and I was struck dumb. I could only see her beauty and wish I were dead. I looked at the child, limp in her arms. As sick as she was, she was a replica of her mother, red hair, freckles sprinkled across her nose and cheeks. But her eyes were brown. My eyes. The child suddenly stiffened as if her disease could take her at any moment. She stared at me with those brown eyes glazed over with sickness.

"'You,' Evangeline said as our eyes met. I pushed the door wide to allow her entrance and then closed it behind her and led her to a chair. She sat down, holding the child close to her. Tersely she told me no one would baptize her daughter. 'The Church will not recognize an innocent child's right to be baptized?' she asked. 'It is not the child's fault I am not married, and I refuse to divulge the father's name. And don't try to talk to me about original sin, venial sin, or mortal sin'.

"I struggled with myself. This was my child, the product of our love, but I could never admit it to another human being. To excuse myself, I said, 'It's against church policy. I cannot do it.'

"'Then you condemn this precious child to purgatory for eternity. Your own little daughter.' She raised her voice and, God help me, I became more concerned about someone outside the door hearing the confrontation than about the child's condemnation.

"My voice came out in a hiss as I whispered, 'Nothing about her is dark, like me.'"

Maggie sat bolt upright in her chair. "What? You denied fathering that little girl?"

"I did." His voice broke and he suppressed a sob.

"I need some fresh air." Maggie fled the room.

CHAPTER FORTY-NINE

When Father Matthew caught up with Maggie, she was sitting on the old bench on the front lawn of the monastery. The early evening breeze ruffled her auburn curls and alleviated the oppressive heat. She looked at him, tears running down her cheeks, fury in her eyes. They sat quietly for some time, Father Matthew holding her hand, not saying a word.

Finally Maggie said, "I feel such sadness for my grandmother and her child, and disgust for a priest, a bishop, who could not do what was right. I do not understand how a man of the cloth could so blatantly dishonor the woman who bore his child. I don't understand why he couldn't have baptized that little girl right there. Who would have known? At last I have a very good idea as to why my father left the Church and what he wanted to tell me when he died. He wanted to defend the honor of his mother."

Matthew stood and pulled her to her feet. "Come, Maggie. Let's walk back. You need to come to terms with this. You have to hear the rest of the story."

Together they entered the room and Father Anthony reached out to Maggie with a withered hand. "I want you to know, Maggie, that the moment I saw your grandmother standing in the doorway, I was as much in love with her as ever I had been. I just didn't handle the mess I created very well." Maggie nodded, but didn't look at him. "After she asked me to baptize the child, and I refused, she left without a word. My heart ached. Again I had chosen the Church over my love for Evangeline.

"Two months later I was running in Minnehaha Park, as was still my habit, and I saw her sitting on the bench on the trail we'd walked together. She looked very tired. The joy that was once ever present had left her eyes and all I could see was misery. I stopped and asked after the child, and she told me the child had died, unbaptized, the night I had seen her. Then she turned her agony and her fury on me. She said her only reason for living was now gone, and she could not bear to live without her. But her greatest sorrow was the knowledge that her child had died unbaptized, doomed to purgatory forever.

"'How could you fail your own child? You, a priest, should care about your child and want to take care of her,' she cried. 'You are not fit to be a priest.'

"I cannot describe the pain I felt, the guilt, the regret that I had not stepped up to be that little girl's father and to honor my commitment to her mother. But instead of falling to my knees and begging Evangeline's forgiveness, I lashed back with the words I regret the most. 'You failed her when you seduced a priest.'"

Maggie's hands flew up and her head snapped back, as if she had been slapped, and then she shrieked, "How could you?" Her hands balled up into white-knuckled fists.

Father Matthew stood and put his arm around her shoulders. "Easy, Maggie."

Father Anthony continued. "Evangeline spat at me, showing her contempt, just as you do today. 'You have shattered my faith,' she told me. 'I renounce the Church and everything it stands for.' Then she said, 'I renounce life, itself.'

"I was alarmed, but did not respond. She raised herself wearily to her feet, and that is when I saw the gun, a small caliber .22

which she had been holding in the folds of her skirt. In my shock, I said, 'If you plan to use that on yourself, you must remember you are committing a mortal sin.' She just shook her head and began to sob. I stepped toward her, aching to give her comfort, but she waved me off. 'Don't come near me,' she said, and then repeated, 'Get away! Get away!'

"I turned back the way I had come, but after a few steps I heard that unmistakable metal on metal clash as she cocked the pistol. Terrified that she was about to take her own life, I wheeled around to stop her. But instead of seeing her turn the gun against herself, I saw her raise her arm and aim the gun toward me. I turned and ran."

Maggie gasped. "It was my grandmother," she whispered.

"Yes, my dear." The old man's voice was raspy and weak. "I have relived the moment every day of my life in that wheelchair. My spine was shattered, you see, and I never walked again." He paused, giving Maggie time to process the awful truth she had worked so hard to find. Her face was frozen in disbelief.

"I know I will have a discussion with St. Peter about my life and my choices. I've done good things for many people, just not for the person I loved the most. The one thing I could do for her was to protect her from the law. I never told a living soul who fired the shot. Until now." He heaved a great sigh. "And I forgave her."

Maggie found her voice, but it was weak, forced past the swelling in her throat. "The person you loved the most shot you in the back," she said. "And you forgave her."

"A thousand times over, my child. I have longed these many years to tell her, and to hear words of forgiveness from her."

Maggie turned to the young priest standing beside her. "Oh, Matthew," she said through her tears, her beautiful face contorted in grief. He reached for her hand, wanting only to gather her in his arms.

The old priest spoke. "Father Matthew, please call for the bishop. I am ready for the holy oil."

Father Matthew stepped away from Maggie and took the old man's hand. "Father, would you like me to administer the sacrament? I would be very honored. I brought the oil and book of prayers. It will take me a few minutes to bring them from the car."

"Thank you, Father Matthew. It would give me joy. Maggie, please stay with me."

Maggie looked startled, but nodded and Matthew left the room. When he returned he was surprised to see Maggie sitting on the edge of the old man's bed, holding his hand. She was telling him about her grandmother's flowers.

Father Matthew leaned over the old priest. "Is there anything else you want to confess, Father?"

"I have made the confession I have needed to make all my life. I am now prepared for death." Matthew continued with the sacrament. He picked up the bowl of oil, but as he began the Prayer of Absolution. Father Anthony held up his hand and gestured toward Maggie.

Father Matthew understood and placed the bowl in Maggie's hands. Her tears mingled with the oil as he completed the sacrament. Her forgiveness was complete as well. At that moment Father Matthew knew his decision was made.

"Is there anything else we can do to make you comfortable, Father?" Matthew asked.

There is one more thing."

"Go on, Father Anthony."

"After I became paralyzed, my assistant, Father John, was very attentive. His considerable skills enabled me to continue with my duties. But he was more ambitious than a dutiful priest should be, and I did not understand this in time to prevent what happened."

"And what was that, Father?"

"Over the years he had unearthed certain documents and put them together with the tragic story presented by the young woman who came, begging, to have her daughter baptized. He surmised, correctly, my secret. He began to urge me to retire. When his urgency became annoying to me, I chastised him, and that's when he told me he knew the truth. He said he would not divulge it if I would agree to retire and endorse him as the next bishop of the diocese. I am ashamed that I permitted him to commit the sin of blackmail. Father Matthew, please ask Bishop Davis to forgive me."

CHAPTER FORTY-SIX

After Maggie left him at the cathedral, Father Matthew went to Father Francesco's cottage. The old priest opened the door, looking quizzical, a thin smile on his lips. "You appear to be on a mission. Is there something else?"

"I don't know how to say this. I am torn between loving the priesthood and loving a woman. Our age-old dichotomy."

Father Francesco laughed, but his eyes remained serious. "It is. You are about to leave the priesthood." It was a statement not a question.

Father Matthew took a deep breath, "I want to be released from my vows, but I want to retain my collar. I know I can love both Maggie and the Church. I know I can be a good priest and a good husband and father."

"Does Maggie know of your decision?"

"No. But I will tell her tomorrow."

"You know you must write a letter to the pope and it will take years to get a response from the Vatican. So the question is, are you and she willing to wait?"

"Two years. No more. If the Vatican denies my request, I will leave the Church without looking back."

The old priest smiled and touched Matthew's bowed head. "I bless your decision."

"Will you help me with the letter?"

"I will. I will also add to my Vatican paper the need for the Church to see that there should be choices for priests. You are not the first, Matthew, to ask this question. Many have left the priesthood for marriage and they have been excommunicated. A sin in itself, I think. Enough of my ramblings. Now let's get a letter written. I will add my endorsement."

CHAPTER FORTY-SEVEN

The letter sent, Father Matthew called Maggie. It was late, but he knew she would be awake. "How about a ride back to Grand Coulee in the morning?" he asked.

"Of course!"

"Meet me in the Holy Names chapel at eight AM.

"Isn't that a bit brazen," she asked, "to drive off together in front of God *and* the bishop?"

"Priests aren't supposed to hitchhike," he laughed.

"Eight AM it is. I'll pick up scones for the road."

Maggie spent a restless night, but for the first time in years, it was neither Aunt Milly nor Grandmother Callahan interfering with her sleep and peace of mind. That was over, she knew, when she forgave the dying priest. It was as close as he would get to Evangeline's forgiveness, and it was enough. Enough, too, for Evangeline who had needed to grant forgiveness. And for Milly who had fiercely loved her little sister but had failed to protect her from the betrayal that could have destroyed their lives. They, too, were at peace.

No, Maggie was discomfited by the truth that she would have to walk out of Matthew's life, and she was not sure how she would cope with it.

Maggie arrived at the cathedral early. She sat in the back pew of the magnificent nave and made a stab at praying she would be able to control her emotions when she said goodbye to Matthew. But she was jerked out of her reverent state when the man with the windbreaker jacket suddenly appeared, fully robed and without the jacket. He saw her and tried to dart back into the room behind the chancel.

"You!" Her voice echoed across the sacred space. "Father, why were you following us? I know it was you at the base camp and at Lake Pateros. Did Bishop Davis send you to spy on us?"

The priest scuffled toward her, his head down. "I can't tell you," he whispered, *sotto voiced*. "You must speak with Father Francesco."

"Father Francesco? What does he have to do with this?" She did not lower her voice.

"I cannot say." He hurried out as Father Matthew approached.

"That man was spying on us," Maggie raged.

"Who? Father Toby?"

"Whatever his name is, I just accused him of working for the bishop, but he said I must speak with Father Francesco. What do you know about this?"

"I know nothing. Honestly. But give me a few minutes. I'll call Father Francesco."

Waiting for Matthew to return, Maggie struggled to stifle her tears. Her anger with another priest just added to her misery. On top of the anger, she knew this was the last time she would see Father Matthew. Her heart ached for wanting a life with him. She thought about all they had been through during their short time together—the fire, the revelation of her grandmother's love, the hideous betrayal, and finally, the shooting of Father Anthony.

When he returned, she noticed Father Matthew had changed into a black tee-shirt with the usual black slacks. No collar. He got into the driver's seat and said, "Forward. We are turning the key on a new adventure." It shot a barb into her heart that he saw their parting as a new adventure, and she didn't trust herself to respond.

They drove, and Matthew talked about nothing that mattered—the potholes, the crops, the animals. Finally Maggie recovered enough from her hurt feelings to ask what he had learned about Father Toby and why he'd been spying on her. Father Matthew laughed. "You aren't going to believe this. He wasn't spying on you, he was spying on me. Father Francesco sent him. It seems Father Francesco thought I might break my vow."

"What?" Maggie blushed. She knew what vow he was talking about. "So he was concerned about your celibacy?"

"I believe he was. I don't know what Father Toby was supposed to do. Charge into the room and throw a bunting between us?" They laughed hysterically at the image of what Father Toby would be obliged to do.

Through hiccups Maggie asked, "Which of us would be most embarrassed?"

"Father Toby, of course." That set up another round of laughter.

The rest of the drive was pleasant. She spent much of the time talking about her new work and what she would do about Narnia and Jon. Narnia's owner had not yet been identified.

"I made a promise to both of them, and I think the answer is to board Narnia near Seattle where Jon can see her often. I love that little horse almost as much as Jon does," she laughed. She kept up the chatter in order to keep herself from thinking about the parting that loomed ahead.

When they arrived in Grand Coulee, Father Matthew pulled the car into the driveway of St. Francis Church and Maggie braced herself. "Maggie, please wait a few minutes. I need to run in and see if there are any messages."

He went into the church and ten minutes later he was back. "First, Father Anthony died last night. I am told it was a peaceful passing."

Maggie was pensive. "I owe him for so much."

"Are you up for a walk up B Street before you leave? The birds seem particularly happy today."

Maggie got out of the car, wondering why she was prolonging the inevitable pain.

They followed B Street to the top of the hill. "Nothing much left, except a few jack rabbits and, I suspect, a rattlesnake or two. It's hard to imagine the restaurants and the boarding houses and brothels that used to line this street," Maggie observed.

"The history of Grand Coulee resides on this street, but there's nothing much to show for it," Father Matthew agreed. "One story is that they didn't bother with sewer systems. Everything just rolled into Rattlesnake Canyon. They call it Poop Lagoon now," he chuckled. The grass is always green out there, so it's a good place for a picnic as long as you stay upwind."

Maggie wondered if he'd brought her up here to make sure she knew about Poop Lagoon.

At the top of the dust-blown hill Father Matthew, out of view of the homes, reached out and took Maggie's hands. Maggie pulled back. It was too painful to let him touch her. Tears formed in her eyes and she didn't want him to see her cry. She turned her head so he couldn't see her anguish and pretended to look out over the dam. Damn the priesthood, she thought.

"Mary Margaret Callahan."

She drew in a deep breath and slightly turned her head toward him. "Yes?"

"I have something for you. I hope you will read it and keep it by your side." He pulled out an envelope and handed it to her. She tore it open and read.

How many times will we walk these hills
seek shells and fossils of a million years
smell sage in ice formed rock
watch the fading sunlight silhouette lace images in our minds
come walk with me in this broad expanse

> *touch dry grass, new flowers, old trees*
> *hear the cacophony of birds*
> *play music in our heads*
> *when rain comes, foreshadowed by dark clouds and wind*
> *when night brushes away the clouds to open up the skies to all*
> *eternity*
> *remember my love*
> *curl yourself around me until our promise can be fulfilled*

Maggie raised her eyes to his, not caring that tears cascaded down her cheeks. "It's beautiful," was all she could say. She wanted to put her arms around him, kiss him, feel his arms around her.

"Maggie, I've asked to be released from my vows. In the same letter to the pope I asked for permission to retain my collar. I wish to remain a priest. If it is not allowed, so be it. I wish to go with you into the future."

Maggie blinked and wiped at her eyes as his words washed over her. "What are you saying?"

"I'm saying in the short time we've been together I know you are the person with whom I want to share this life. I cannot discuss marriage at this time, because I don't know how long it will take for the Vatican to respond to my letter. The letter clearly states that I will wait only two years."

Maggie inhaled, trying not to choke on her tears. Half crying, half laughing, she asked, "Am I allowed to touch you or must I wait for a papal dispensation?"

Father Matthew laughed, reached out and held her tight as they kissed. "Is that the answer to your question?" he whispered. They stood, wrapped in each other's embrace, swaying to the music of the summer breeze and birdsong.

Maggie finally broke the magical moment with one of her common sense questions. "How will this work?" she asked.

"I don't want to follow in Bishop Anthony's footsteps, Maggie. It may be a long time until I can hold you and we can be together, before I can make proper love to you, but I hope you will wait. I want you as a part of my life. I tell you, Maggie Callahan, you are the love of my life. I wish we'd met earlier, because now we have hurdles to overcome, the first being that you must live alone until I'm free. The second is that I may not hold you in public places and there may not be many opportunities for us to be alone."

She nodded her understanding, and he went on.

"I hope you will live in Grand Coulee and reinvent your Catholic spirit. Once I'm released, we'll go where you can follow your dreams. If I'm able to retain my collar, I will serve the Church in whatever way is possible." Matthew took her hands and kissed her fingers. In a whisper he said, "Mary Margaret Callahan, I love you."

"Oh, Matthew, I have to admit I'm scared. How can I keep my face from telling everyone I'm in love with you?" With a mischievous twinkle in her eye, she said, "If we tell no one else, we must tell Father Francesco. He can keep a secret."

"We have Father Francesco's blessing. He helped me draft the letter directly to the pope, bypassing the bishop."

"What did he say when you told him?"

Father Matthew smiled. "He laughed out loud and I didn't get the joke. He knew exactly what I wanted to say when I walked through the door. He agrees with my decision. He's written an attachment to my request, recommending that I be allowed to retain my collar. Perhaps this will set a precedent. I hope so."

Maggie looked at this man she loved. "My head is reeling. There is so much to think about. Yes, I will wait. Yes I will live here, but I'll need a place for Narnia. I need to call Jon and tell him we have a horse, and—"

Laughing, Matthew stopped her, kissing her again. "One thing at a time."

"Just one more thing," she whispered, pulling his head down to her lips.

"Matthew Brannigan, I love you."

Together they walked down the hill into their new adventure.

ACKNOWLEDGEMENTS

Writing this book was a journey. It has been in my head for over fifty years. Writers talk about their self-doubt, fear, and joy when they birth a book. I experienced all these emotions, plus how will it ever be good enough to print. A special thanks to all of you who asked how the book was moving along.

First readers Jack and Bea Rawls, Mimi Marshal, Mike Hardy, Nancy Hazelton, Ann Adams, Kathy Parks, Harry Sloan, and my late brother Scott, who all tore it apart so I could put it back together. Thank you for keeping me focused.

To Birdie at the Grand Coulee Dam Museum who opened the door to me so I could research.

To the Honcha ladies, Micky Coleman, Margaret Bendet, Donna Hood, Dorothy Read, and Linda Russell, readers and writers extraordinaire.

A special thanks to my editor, Dorothy Read, who had faith in the story and made it a fine read. With her eternal optimism, she lifted me from doubts and dark moments.

And a big thanks to Bob for support, especially at the computer, and several readings looking for those last little errors.

BIOGRAPHY

Pat Kelley Brunjes is a retired librarian, school administrator, and educator who dedicated her career to teaching students the arts of speaking, writing, and acting. While continuing to mentor young writers and actors, she now teaches writing, poetry, and public-speaking skills to adults. She also organizes writing conferences and retreats in addition to focusing on her own work.

Brunjes, an award-winning poet, previously published *Poetry from the Desert Floor*, a collection of photographs and poems reflecting her love of the Southwest and the people who live there. *The Last Confession* is her first mystery novel.

Wh163y220

Made in the USA
Lexington, KY
28 March 2017